With Just One Wing

ALSO BY BRENDA WOODS

With Just One Wing

BRENDA WOODS

NANCY PAULSEN BOOKS

NANCY PAULSEN BOOKS
An imprint of Penguin Random House LLC, New York

First published in the United States of America by Nancy Paulsen Books,
an imprint of Penguin Random House LLC, 2024

Visit us online at PenguinRandomHouse.com.

Library of Congress Cataloging-in-Publication Data
Names: Woods, Brenda (Brenda A.), author. | Title: With just one wing / Brenda Woods.
Description: New York: Nancy Paulsen Books, 2024. | Summary: While nursing a broken arm,
almost-twelve-year-old adoptee Coop, with the help of his grandfather and friend Zandi,
unwaveringly cares for and protects Hop, a baby mockingbird born with one wing.
Identifiers: LCCN 2023034858 | ISBN 9780593461532 (hardcover) |
ISBN 9780593461549 (ebook) | Subjects: CYAC: Adopted children—Fiction. | Animal rescue—
Fiction. | Mockingbirds—Fiction. | Birds—Fiction. | Animals with disabilities—Fiction. | Family
life—Fiction. | African Americans—Fiction.
Classification: LCC PZ7.W86335 Wi 2024 | DDC [Fic]—dc23
LC record available at https://lccn.loc.gov/2023034858

Printed in the United States of America

ISBN 9780593461532

1st Printing
LSCH

Edited by Nancy Paulsen
Design by Eileen Savage | Text set in Adobe Caslon Pro

For my family—present and past

With Just One Wing

What I want to be true

SHE STARED INTO my eyes and kissed my cheeks. But she was sad because, for some reason, she couldn't keep her newborn baby boy—me.

What is true

THE HOSPITAL EMERGENCY room was where she brought me when I was only one day old, making me a Safe Haven Baby and a Ward of the State. I was given a number instead of a name.

My foster parents, Thelonious and Willow Garnette, took me home with them the very next day. They decided to adopt me right away, but it would take almost a year before I was no longer a Ward of the State. In front of a judge, my adoption was finally made official, and I became Cooper Jaxon Garnette—a.k.a. Coop.

1

Almost Twelve Years Later, Los Angeles, California
The First Monday of Summer Break

"COOP!" POPS HOLLERED.

I moaned and pulled the covers over my head.

"Coop! Up! Now! I can't be late for rehearsal!"

If Mom were here, I would have been able to catch a few more summertime z's, but on Saturday she headed off to the San Francisco Conservatory of Music to teach piano in their summer youth program, like she does every summer. I yawned and stretched.

A very loud whistle was his third warning, and having no choice, I rolled out of bed.

In no time, I was dressed, heading to the car, chomping on one of my pops' homemade breakfast burritos, and sipping on some OJ. Like the prized possession it was, he carefully slid his trombone onto the back seat, and we were off to G-Pop and Nana Garnette's place.

Los Angeles, like me, was now wide awake, and as usual, morning traffic was bumper-to-bumper. I checked out my pops as he drove. Today, he was wearing lime-green jeans, a bright Hawaiian button-down shirt, purple suspenders, polka-dot socks, and geometric checkerboard Vans. The way he dresses used to embarrass me until he explained that playing in the Los Angeles Philharmonic orchestra for a living, where he could only wear black and white, had transformed him into someone who dressed in a magical way whenever he wasn't working.

As for me, there was nothing magical about the way I dressed. In fact, there was nothing magical about me at all. I, Coop Garnette, was just a regular kid in almost every way. And unlike the rest of my family, I was not musical at all. No matter how hard I tried, I just wasn't. I even sang way off-key, and trying to learn to read music had been like trying to read hieroglyphics. There were times when I thought that maybe I'd been adopted into the wrong family and worried that the Garnettes were secretly disappointed that they hadn't gotten a kid who was magical or at least musical.

Like he normally does when he drives, Pops was

singing along with some old-school music on the radio. As I stared out the window, I looked forward to tonight's game with the Meteors, my youth b-ball team. Last week, I'd surprised everyone, including myself, with my first ever three-pointer. I pictured a repeat and smiled.

2

WE PULLED UP to the curb. Nana, my pops' mom, who was working in the garden of her duplex, saw us and smiled her big smile.

"See ya, Pops," I said as I climbed out of the car.

"Later, Coop," he replied, and after saying, "Hey," to Nana, he zoomed away.

She peeled off her gardening gloves, planted a kiss on my forehead, and together we headed upstairs to the second story, where they live. As usual, jazz music was playing.

G-Pop, short for Grandpop, was sitting on the back balcony, sipping coffee. He smiled and asked the same question he normally does when he first sees me. "How's my favorite grandson today?"

As usual, I replied, "I'm your only grandson."

His next line was "And therefore, my favorite." Finally, like always, we butted knuckles.

G-Pop shook his head and chuckled. "I think we need to come up with a different jive, Coop."

I knew what he meant. "Yeah, I think so too."

"The next time I see you, I'm gonna greet you with some brand-new jive."

"I'll believe that when I hear it," Nana said playfully, then asked, "You had breakfast, Coop?"

"Just ate," I told her.

I had started to head to the den to play video games when G-Pop said, "Before you rush off to that game cave, there's something you oughta see."

"What?"

"That northern mockingbird finally laid her eggs."

Since G-Pop retired earlier this year, he'd started playing at bird-watching. Nana called it playing because she claimed it was the same as the way he'd been amusing himself with his five-string banjo most of his life, just enough to get a nice bit of enjoyment from it.

At first I had absolutely zero interest in birds, but G-Pop had gotten me and Zandi, the girl who lives downstairs, curious. Together we'd watched the two birds gather twigs and other stuff to build their nest in the tall backyard tree.

G-Pop handed me his binoculars. "Have a look-see, Coop. They're as pretty as can be."

I adjusted the binoculars until the nest came into focus. There they were, four mockingbird eggs, light blue with brown blotches.

"Why are they called mockingbirds, anyway?" I asked.

"Because they mimic other birds and sounds. They're musicians of sorts."

"Do you think they built their nest here because they like listening to your music?"

"Hadn't thought about that, Coop, but you just might be right."

I stared intently at the eggs.

"Well, well, well, Coop Garnette, would you look at us. Seems like we've gone and become gen-u-wine bird watchers. In about two weeks, according to my research, we should have us some hatchlings to spy on."

"Zandi has to see them!" I exclaimed, and dashed to the door. Zandi is a little older than me, and her mom rents the downstairs unit from G-Pop and Nana. I rang and knocked but no one answered. Disappointed, I headed upstairs and went back outside onto the balcony.

Patiently, I watched and waited and waited some more until one of the birds finally came back to the nest and sat on the eggs. "G-Pop," I said, "he's sitting on the eggs."

"That's called incubation," he explained, "and only a mama mockingbird incubates, so it's a she."

"Oh . . . the mama . . . she."

Suddenly my birth mother popped into my mind, the way she does now and then. It was probably seeing that mama bird sitting on her eggs that made it happen this time. I asked myself the usual questions. *Where is she, somewhere close by or far away? Does she ever think about me? Would I recognize her if I saw her? Would she recognize me?*

3

HOURS LATER, THE Atlanta Braves, G-Pop's favorite baseball team, were playing the Houston Astros, and he was pacing back and forth in front of the television, shouting at the umpire, the way he does whenever his team is losing.

From the other room, where she was playing her cello, Nana hollered, "Calm down, Miles, before you get your blood pressure up!"

He plopped down in his recliner but kept on fussing.

Earlier today, I'd thought about sneaking outside to do something. I, Coop Garnette, had discovered a while back that being successful at sneaking is more likely to occur when no one's watching. And now, with G-Pop and Nana preoccupied, their eyes elsewhere, it seemed like the perfect time.

I really wanted to touch those eggs. No—I had to. I snuck to the door, crept downstairs, and hightailed it to the backyard.

Because I'm pretty good at climbing, I figured it'd be a cinch. I pulled myself up to the first branch and then the next and then the one above that. "Just don't look down, Coop," I told myself, and kept going. At last, the nest was within reach.

And just as I was about to touch the eggs, Zandi yelled out from below, "Coop, what're you doing way up there?!"

"The bird laid her eggs! They're incredibly amazing! C'mon up, it's easy! Don't be scared, Zandi!"

"I am not scared!" she said, and began climbing.

Then, suddenly, from out of nowhere it appeared— one of the mockingbirds, flying straight at me, squawking its head off. To avoid a collision, I ducked, and moments later, when it swooped again, just missing me, I swatted at it and screamed, "Cut it out!"

"That is one mad bird, Coop! You should come down fast, before you get hurt!" Zandi warned.

I was about to take her advice when the mockingbirds

double-teamed me. I tried my best to avoid them, leaning this way and that. But in the end, it was unavoidable, and down I went.

Zandi screamed.

Seconds later, I crash-landed, and it was lights-out for Coop Garnette.

4

THE FIRST THING that woke up were my ears, and I heard a siren blaring. Then Nana asked, "Can you hear me, Coop?" I tried to answer but couldn't talk.

Suddenly, my eyes opened. I was inside an ambulance. A paramedic was there with my nana, and there was some kind of brace around my neck.

Nana was holding my hand. "I'm right here, Coop," she said softly.

But my tongue still wasn't working, and when I tried to move my body, I couldn't do that either. Before long, my eyes closed, and it was lights-out again.

THE NEXT TIME I woke up, I was inside some kind of noisy machine that was making a clicking sound. My mind was wonky, scrambled like eggs, and I imagined this contraption was taking me to heaven. I opened my mouth, and this time words came out. "Is anybody there?" I asked. "Am I dead or alive?"

"Definitely alive," a man replied. "Try and be still, Cooper. You're having a scan. We're almost done."

AS THE LIGHT bulb inside my brain flickered on and off, I thought a day that was going to turn into this kind of fiasco should have come with a warning from the Emergency Alert System or some other kind of tip-off, but it hadn't. Was this going to be the end of Coop Garnette?

I battled hard to stay awake but ultimately lost, and at that point, they would later tell me, I sank into a coma—a period of prolonged unconsciousness brought on by illness or, in my case, a serious injury.

5

Two Days Later

"COOP. WAKE UP, dude. C'mon, Coop, please." I knew that voice; it was Pops.

I tried and tried to open my eyes until finally I succeeded.

Mom was there too, and the way they started whooping and hollering, you would have thought it was New Year's Eve. And then the crying started.

My voice was raspy. "What happened?" I looked around. "Why am I in the hospital?"

They glanced at each other. "You fell out of the tree, Coop. Do you remember?" Pops asked.

I stared at them blankly.

Tears rolled down Mom's cheeks. "You climbed up to see the nest."

I dug deep into my memory until I began to find bits and pieces of what had happened. "Oh . . . yeah, now I remember. I was trying to touch the eggs." But the next thing I recalled made me cringe. "Then the birds attacked me, right?"

They nodded.

I tried to sit up, but my head hurt and I felt woozy.

"Careful, Coop. You have a concussion, and you've been in a coma," Pops informed me.

"Coma?"

Mom kissed me and wiped at her tears while she explained. "You had a skull fracture and an open compound fracture of your right radius and ulna."

"Huh?"

Pops translated. "You cracked your skull when you fell. Plus, you broke your arm and had to have surgery."

I felt my head. It was bandaged, and my right arm was in a cast. It was time for me to man up. "Give it to me straight, I can handle it. Am I gonna die?"

"No, Coop, you're not gonna die, but you'll have to take it easy for a while," Pops replied.

I was searching his eyes, hoping he was telling me the truth, when the doctors arrived.

Most of the tests they gave me were pretty easy, and the doctor said I passed them with flying colors.

"The good news is," she reported, "there's no hematoma, which means a blood clot, and there doesn't appear to be any permanent brain damage. Your memory of the actual event is fuzzy, but that's not uncommon with injuries like this. So far, no seizures, so that's good too."

The bad news was I had to stay in the hospital for a few more days to be observed, just in case.

"You were very lucky, Coop," the doctor told me. "This could have been much worse. If I were you, I'd do my bird-watching from a safe place. And I'd definitely stay out of trees."

Later, G-Pop and Nana showed up to visit, and Zandi came with her mom too. And that night, Pops slept there beside me in a reclining chair and Mom on a fold-up bed. But because I was afraid they might never open again, I was scared to close my eyes. Eventually, though, no matter how hard I tried to keep sleep from coming, it came anyway.

When I woke up the next morning, I smiled and felt that feeling called happiness.

Unfortunately, that feeling didn't last very long, because when I sat up on the side of the bed, my whole body felt like one humongous ache. And when Pops helped me to go to the bathroom and I saw my reflection in the mirror, the image that stared back at me was horrifying! My face was so bruised and swollen that I almost didn't look like Coop Garnette. Instead, I resembled a hideous movie zombie.

Pops got that I-feel-for-you-bro look in his eyes and gave me a shoulder hug.

"Ouch!"

"Sorry!"

My legs were wobbly like they'd forgotten how to hold me up. But slowly, with help from Pops, I made it back to bed. I, Coop Garnette, was used to spending hours on the court, but right then I was so tired, I felt like I could sleep for a hundred years.

After breakfast, Pops headed home to shower before orchestra practice, and Mom and I were alone when I asked, "Isn't this the same hospital where—"

Mom interrupted, "Where I first held you? . . . Yes, it is."

"I was gonna ask, where she brought me?"

"Yes, Coop. This is the same hospital. She brought you

to a safe place and gave us a greater gift than we could have ever asked for."

"Right now, I'm a really banged-up gift."

Mom smiled and gently squeezed my hand. "Before you know it, you'll be as good as new."

I hoped she was right.

6

ONCE I WAS back home, Pops, G-Pop, and Nana tried their best to convince Mom to go back to her summer job in San Francisco, but she wasn't having it. So there I was, a righty with a broken right arm, struggling to do basic stuff like get dressed and go to the bathroom and having to do odd things like sit on a chair to shower with my cast wrapped in a plastic bag. Adding to my misery, I was stuck at home with grown-ups worrying way too much about me, hovering around like helicopters, their noses in everything I did. If I sneezed, they practically jumped out of their skins, and once I was able to get to the bathroom on my own, they still insisted on standing guard outside the door. Twice, I'd tried to sneak outside to sit on the backyard patio by myself, just to be alone. But there were always too many eyes on Coop Garnette.

Some people claimed that me even being alive was some kind of miracle. But I was looking forward to the day when being alive was like it had been before—easy.

My head had finally stopped hurting, but because there were times when my mind felt a little foggy, I worried that my brain might never be the same. No matter how hard I tried, I still couldn't remember the actual fall. But fortunately, I could recall everything else that had happened in my life. I flashed back to the three-pointer I'd made during my last basketball game and hoped it wouldn't be my one and only.

Making things even worse, my best friend, Karlan, was spending the summer in Texas with his father, so he wasn't there to clown around, make me laugh, and take away some of the boringness of my predicament. But we'd been able to FaceTime on the computer, and when he first saw me, he said the same thing I'd thought: "Oh man, Coop, you look like you walked straight out of a zombie movie."

"Yeah, I know. And I kinda feel like one too," I told him.

Some of the rest of my crew and the boys on my basketball team came to visit, and I wanted to believe them when they said, "Don't worry, dude, you'll be back on the court with the Meteors in no time," and promised to see me soon. But they were mostly busy with practice, games, and other summertime fun stuff, so they really weren't interested in being cooped up with Coop Garnette.

I ran my fingers along my forehead where the stitches had been. The scab was itchy, but so far, I'd kept my promise not to scratch. Would the scar be there forever, a constant reminder of my fiasco, or would it gradually fade away?

The doctor kept talking about the speedy recovery I was making. But in my opinion, there was nothing speedy about it. Instead, I felt like a turtle who was slowly inching toward a distant finish line.

I was staring at the ceiling, counting the days until my cast was supposed to come off, when Mom came in and asked if I wanted to go to G-Pop and Nana's while she ran some errands. Of course, I jumped at the chance.

For the first time ever, climbing their stairs wasn't a breeze, and I had to take one step at a time and hold on to the railing to keep my balance. But when I finally made it, Zandi was there too, smiling one of those smiles that forces you to smile back.

"You sure look a whole lot better than you did when you were in the hospital," she said.

"Thanks."

"Glad you didn't die, Coop."

"Me too."

"How's my favorite grandson?" G-Pop asked.

"Didn't I warn you he wasn't gonna have any brand-new jive?" Nana teased.

G-Pop laughed. "Guilty as charged."

"The baby mockingbirds are starting to hatch!" Zandi exclaimed. "Wanna see?"

She offered me the binoculars, but birds were the last thing on my mind. "I hate those birds! They double-teamed me, and that's why I fell! I coulda died! I don't ever wanna see any stinking birds again for as long as I live!"

Zandi cracked a smile. "That'd be kinda impossible, since birds are pretty much everywhere."

"They were only doing their job, Coop, protecting their nest," G-Pop explained. "They attacked you because *you* were an interloper."

"What's an interloper?" I asked.

"Someone who pokes their nose in where it doesn't belong."

Zandi stared through the binoculars. "Another one's hatching, Coop! You gotta see!"

I really didn't want to, but she was so excited that I gave in. One of the baby birds was almost completely out of its shell and another was just beginning. Spying on birds really was fascinating, I thought. Plus, G-Pop was right, it wasn't their fault I had been an interloper.

"How long before they can fly?" I asked him.

"Two or three more weeks," he replied. "First, the hatchlings become nestlings. Then, once they grow feathers and leave the nest, they're called fledglings."

"And when they're fledglings, they can fly?"

"Yes . . . they'll be ready for takeoff."

I stared at the nest. "I wanna see that . . . when they learn to fly."

Zandi poked fun. "Thought you hated birds, Coop."

"Be quiet, Zandi."

1

NATURALLY I BEGGED to go back to G-Pop and Nana's again, not just to bird-watch but to hang out with Zandi, who was staying with them on the days when her mom was working.

Zandi opened the door and announced, "They've all hatched!" So right away we settled in for some serious bird-spying.

She handed me the binoculars, but because I could only use one hand, I had trouble focusing. Zandi had to help me get my first glimpses of the four nestlings. "Where'd the eggshells go?" I asked.

"Sometimes they take pieces and carry them away, or the mom bird actually eats them to replace the calcium she used to make the eggshells in the first place. I learned that online last night."

"Seems like eggshells would be hard to swallow," I told her.

She giggled. "For real, huh. Know what else I found out?"

"What?"

"Some birds actually lay their eggs in other birds' nests."

"Why would they wanna do that? So they don't have to build a nest of their own?"

"Probably," she replied. "Or maybe they want someone else to adopt their egg because they don't wanna take care of it themselves."

Sometimes when a person makes the word *adopt* sound like a bad thing, I feel a little weird inside, so I get very quiet and stare blankly. This was one of those times.

"Whatsamatter, Coop?" Zandi asked.

"I'm adopted," I revealed.

"Sorry, Coop. I didn't know, or I wouldn't have said that."

"It's okay."

"Thanks for telling me—why didn't you ever tell me before?"

I shrugged. "I dunno. It's not a secret or anything. My mom and pops told me a long time ago when I was little."

Zandi took a deep breath before she asked, "Do you know who your birth parents are?"

"No," I replied, and told her about being brought to the hospital.

A long, uncomfortable silence preceded her next question. "Do you ever think about finding them, your birth family?"

"Yeah, sometimes. But it might be impossible."

"Why?"

I explained what being a Safe Haven Baby meant, that people could choose not to give a name or contact information and that my birth mother had chosen to do just that—to be anonymous.

Zandi took another deep breath. "Do your other friends know?"

"Mostly. They're chill about it."

She smiled. "I'm chill too. Besides, it really doesn't matter how you get into a family. Plus, at least your mom and pops wanted you and didn't havta get tricked into it by somebody laying an egg in their nest."

I was picturing myself as an egg that had wound up in someone else's nest when Nana started playing her cello.

"I wish I could play an instrument like everyone else in my family, but I'm a complete zero at music."

"Me too," Zandi confided. "I took piano lessons, but it was a disaster."

"Same," I confessed. "I've tried almost every instrument there is, even the tuba, and all of them were hard."

"Maybe we should try the tambourine or the cymbals."

"Or that triangle thing," I added.

Nana began playing a song that was so pretty, I stopped talking to listen. Zandi must have thought so too, because she said, "I like hearing your nana play and listening to G-Pop's jazz albums. Sometimes, from downstairs, I hear their music and I dance. At least dancing is something I'm really good at."

I lifted my broken arm. "Yeah, and I was getting pretty good at basketball until . . ."

Some noise from the mockingbirds turned our attention back to them. One by one, the little nestlings were being fed. When we focused closely, we discovered that their feathers were sprouting. I could hardly wait to see them fly.

8

A FEW NIGHTS later I woke up shivering, but my head was burning up. Feeling hot and cold at the same time only meant one thing: Coop Garnette was sick.

I dragged myself to my parents' room.

Mom, half-asleep, asked, "What's wrong, Coop?"

"I dunno, I just don't feel good."

Pops woke up. "What's going on?"

"My arm really hurts, and I don't feel good."

Mom, now wide awake, said, "Sit down, Coop. Let me take your temperature."

When the thermometer beeped, I could tell by her expression that it wasn't good news. "It's 102.9," she told Pops, and the Coop-has-a-fever routine began. First, they gave me medicine to bring down the fever. That part, I was very familiar with. Step two, as usual, was to make me lie down with a cool facecloth on my head. The next thing they did wasn't a part of the regular routine, but I figured that was because of my recent fiasco—they called the doctor.

"Yes, his arm hurts . . . No, he doesn't have a headache," Pops told the doctor when he called back. And what happened next was a brand-new thing. Quickly, they got dressed and rushed me to the hospital emergency room.

"I'm kinda getting sick of hospitals," I confessed while we waited for the doctor.

Mom patted my shoulder, and Pops was fidgeting the way he does when he's worried. Even though I was feeling bad, for some reason his purple-and-blue-plaid pants and orange-dotted shirt made me smile.

When we finally got into the emergency room, someone came and took my blood, three tubes to be exact, and then someone else sawed the cast off. The wound was oozing smelly greenish pus. I gagged and almost threw up.

"It looks infected," the doctor said, "but if we're lucky, it's not in the bone."

"And if we're not lucky?" Pops asked.

"Let's wait for the blood work to come back before we start to worry. In the meantime, I'll order a scan."

Soon I was back inside the same noisy machine as before. At least this time I knew that I wasn't on my way to heaven. "Be as still as you can, Cooper," said the lady who was operating the machine.

"You can call me Coop," I told her. "Most people do."

"Okay, be very still, Coop."

While we waited in the emergency room for the test results, I fell asleep. When I woke up, Mom and Pops were smiling. "The infection's not in the bone, Coop. Just the wound."

"So now what?"

"They're going to start you on antibiotics. And you'll have a splint instead of the cast so we can keep an eye on the wound and keep it clean," Mom answered.

And now for the most important question of all. "Do I have to stay in the hospital?"

"No, you can go home."

Coop Garnette breathed a huge sigh of relief.

9

BECAUSE OF MY latest hospital adventure, the next time I asked Mom to take me to G-Pop and Nana's, she hesitated. But I was feeling caged up again and wanted out. Plus, I wasn't about to miss seeing those baby birds learn to fly. So I begged.

"Please, Mom," I pleaded, "I havta see them fly." I smiled as pleasantly as I could until, finally, she said okay.

As soon as I got there, Zandi proudly displayed new high-powered binoculars. "My mom bought them for me."

"Cool."

Nana came out of the kitchen and said, "Hi, Coop."

"Where's G-Pop?" I asked.

"Today's his golf day," she reminded me.

Now that he was retired, he'd promised that this summer he'd get serious about teaching me to golf, but my being an interloper had even changed that. I glanced at my arm and groaned. "No golf for me this summer either, I guess. This accident sure messed everything up."

But Zandi quickly interrupted my poor-me party. "Coop, these binoculars are so powerful you can even see their tiny tongues. You wanna look?"

"That's a ridiculous question, of course I do."

With Zandi's new binoculars, I gazed at the four baby birds, and it felt like I was right there with them in the nest. Each time one of the parent birds came with food, all four little nestlings opened their mouths widely, begging to be fed.

"They sure seem hungry," I told Zandi.

"They are. In fact, baby birds are practically insatiable."

"Huh?"

"They're almost always hungry and have to be fed every fifteen to thirty minutes, except at night when they're sleeping."

"Sure seems like a lot of work for the mom and pop birds. Wonder what they eat?"

Of course, Zandi had the answer. "Seeds and berries mostly, and also worms and insects like crickets or spiders. I've been learning a lot about birds, Coop. It said on the bird website that if we can get live crickets or mealworms to put outside, that'd make it easier for them to find food."

"Crickets would probably just hop away," I told her. "Mealworms seem better."

Zandi agreed, and luckily, there was a pet store nearby.

"I'll drive you," Nana said.

"No, thanks," I told her. "It's only a couple of blocks, and the doctor said it's okay for me to take short walks now."

"I'm coming with you, then," she insisted.

"It's not that far, Nana. We're not little kids."

But there was no persuading her and I knew why. My fiasco had happened when she'd been preoccupied, and she wasn't going to let that happen again.

For the record, mealworms, dead or alive, are not pretty to look at. In fact, they're kind of creepy, and the live ones actually make your skin crawl. But according to the man at the pet store, birds seem to like them better alive, so that's what we bought, along with a mealworm bird feeder.

As soon as we got back, we headed to the yard to set

everything up. It was my first time being there since the accident.

I stared up at the branch I'd fallen from. "Wow . . . I'm amazed I'm alive," I told Zandi.

She said, "So am I."

10

LIKE EVERY YEAR on the Fourth of July, the Garnettes headed to the Hollywood Bowl for the annual Fireworks Spectacular. The Los Angeles Philharmonic, which includes my pops, was playing. G-Pop was driving, with Nana beside him, and Mom was in the back seat with me. Hearing them talk, joke, and laugh as we drove made me extra happy that I'd survived, and it felt good to be doing a normal family thing for the first time in a while. I was glad the doctor had said it was okay for me to go as long as I wore sunglasses to dim the lights from the fireworks.

I was people-watching when I saw her. She rushed to get to the seat right in front of me, and before she sat down, she turned and said, "Hope I'm not blocking your view, young man."

"No, I can see just fine," I replied.

Her eyes twinkled when she stared at me. Then she smiled.

Our skin was almost exactly the same color, and her round face resembled mine. And the way I sometimes did when I saw a woman who looked a lot like me, I wondered, *Could this be her? Could this be the one who'd brought me to the hospital that day? My birth mother?*

Mom, sitting beside me, nudged me and offered me something to eat. Right then, I got a serious case of feeling guilty. Why was I even thinking about *her* when I had a really nice mom who loved me? Shouldn't I be satisfied? I glanced over at Willow Garnette's face.

She gazed up at the stars and asked, "Isn't it a beautiful night, Coop?"

I nodded and smiled.

And when the orchestra began to play and colorful fireworks exploded in the nighttime sky, Mom hugged my shoulder, and I forgot all about that other stuff.

11

Going to G-Pop and Nana's had practically become an everyday thing while I was recuperating from my fiasco. Zandi and I were determined not to miss when the baby mockingbirds took their first flights, and day after day, we watched them, waiting eagerly.

But I was getting impatient. "Aren't they ever gonna fly?"

Zandi sighed. "Seems like it's taking forever."

"You know what you two are suffering from?" G-Pop told us.

"What?"

"A very bad case of 'a watched pot never boils'" was his answer.

"What's that got to do with birds?" Zandi asked.

"It's a wise saying, Zandi. A proverb." G-Pop loved proverbs, and he had one for almost everything. "Means time seems to pass very slowly when you're waiting anxiously for something to happen." He smiled. "But don't worry, there's a cure for it."

"What's the cure, G-Pop?"

"Distraction."

"You mean getting us to think about something else to stop us from thinking about when the birds will fly?" Zandi asked.

"Exactly, and I think I know just the place. As luck would have it, your nana is at the zoo today volunteering in the garden, and she forgot her lunch and asked me to bring it to her. Let's get going."

"But what if the baby birds fly away before we get back?" I asked.

"Highly unlikely. It takes a while for nestlings to leave, and even after they do, they don't stray too far from the nest until they get good at flying. Oh, and bring your binoculars."

"Why?" Zandi asked.

G-Pop replied with only a wink, and in a jiffy, we were off to the Los Angeles Zoo.

We found Nana working in the enrichment garden. "It's a garden where we grow food specifically for the animals," she explained, "and all of the plants are nontoxic from root to leaf." As she continued talking about plants, I couldn't speak for Zandi, but I wasn't exactly feeling distracted.

"Coop and Zandi, how about we head over to the aviary?" G-Pop suggested.

I grinned. Now I knew what the binoculars were for.

We were just about to step inside the aviary when Zandi said, "Don't you think it's kinda sad that birds have to be caged up in here? Seems like it'd be extremely boring for them."

I agreed. "It's sorta like a bird prison."

"But there's a flip side to this coin," G-Pop told us.

Before I could ask what coin he was talking about, he explained.

"That's a saying that means that sometimes there's a completely different way to look at a situation. On the one hand, the birds inside the aviary aren't free to roam and fly wherever they please, but then again, they're safe from predators like cats. Plus, they'll never starve, and some of the endangered ones are saved from becoming extinct.

So there are some good things about zoos and living in captivity."

Zandi frowned, shook her head, and said, "Still seems like birds oughta be free."

I sided with Zandi again. "Yeah, being free's a whole lot better."

G-Pop chuckled. "Well, I can tell I'm not about to win this debate, so how about we do some bird-watching."

The large aviary was home to singing, squawking, and chattering birds. Some flew and soared, while others perched on branches or scuttled across the ground, chirping. With G-Pop's help we identified a bunch of them, including the African spoonbill, the red-billed blue magpie, the violet turaco, and, my favorite of the day, the white-crowned robin-chat.

Like G-Pop had said, being inside the enclosure with the birds was totally distracting.

The cure, however, was only temporary, and when we left the aviary, my thoughts immediately flew back to the nestlings. As we drove to G-Pop's, I kept hoping he'd been right and they hadn't flown away yet. As soon as we got there, we rushed to see. Just as he'd predicted, all four baby mockingbirds were still in the nest.

12

THERE ARE SOME things you can do for countless hours without getting bored, but keeping our eyes on the baby birds and waiting patiently for them to take off flying wasn't one of them. Fortunately, playing video games helped cure our monotony. Once a day, while G-Pop kept his eye on the nestlings, Zandi and I retreated to the game cave.

"I won again!" Zandi bragged.

Before the fiasco, whenever I'd played Zandi, I'd usually been the winner. But now, because I had to play one-handed she kept defeating me, and my confidence was withering.

I waved my broken arm. "A slight disadvantage. Let's see what happens if you play with only one hand. That'll make it fair."

Zandi grinned. "No way, Coop. Finally beating you is too much fun."

"Enjoy it while you can, because when this splint comes off, I will once again reign supreme."

Every day, we'd watch the birds, discover nothing had changed, play video games, then check on the birds again. We even ate lunch on the balcony, pausing frequently to spy on the nestlings.

For days, things were mostly the same—until the day they weren't.

I was barely through the front door when Zandi announced sadly, "Three of them graduated, but we missed it."

"Graduated?" I asked.

"They've left the nest and become fledglings," G-Pop explained.

"All except one. I hope we at least get to see it take off," Zandi said.

"Me too," I told her. Because one was still there, I wasn't totally disappointed.

As I studied the lone baby mockingbird, I began wondering about the other three. G-Pop had told us before that fledglings don't venture too far at first. "So you think the others are still nearby?" I asked him.

"Probably. Let's go look," G-Pop suggested.

Luckily the mom and pop mockingbirds weren't around—not that we could see, anyway. But we were quiet and cautious because we now knew that being unable to spot them didn't mean they weren't lurking close by, ready to attack interlopers. Carefully, we searched the backyard, and before long, we found one of the fledglings perched in some bushes, another in Nana's flower garden, and one more hopping along near the bottom of the tree. We kept a safe distance as we watched them practicing, fluttering their wings, preparing to one day soon soar through the sky.

Thinking it might be any minute before the last one left the nest, we headed back up to the balcony to observe. No way were we missing this final takeoff.

"Wonder why it won't go?" Zandi asked.

"Maybe it's scared," I told her. "I mean, I'd be scared if I'd never flown before."

"So would I," Zandi admitted.

Once more, I zeroed in with my binoculars on the

remaining nestling. And that was when I made a startling discovery. "It only has one wing!" I exclaimed.

Zandi focused on the bird. "You're right, it does."

"How come we never noticed that before?" I asked.

"I dunno."

"G-Pop, Nana!" I yelled. "The last baby bird only has one wing!"

They rushed to see.

G-Pop's face lit up with surprise. "I suppose we couldn't tell with the other birds crowded around it. Well, I'll be, isn't that unique."

"Poor thing," Nana said sadly, "to be born a bird that'll never fly."

"But there are other birds that can't fly, like ostriches, penguins, and kiwis," Zandi informed us.

"Except, unlike most birds, those aren't meant to fly and have adapted to it," G-Pop explained.

I was afraid of the answer to the question I was about to ask but asked anyway. "What's gonna happen to it, G-Pop?"

"It'll likely be abandoned by its parents once they discover it can't fly, or a cat or squirrel might get it, or it'll somehow wriggle itself out of the nest and wind up on the ground," he replied.

Zandi pouted. "So it's gonna starve, fall, or get eaten?"

He patted her shoulder. "Sorry, Zandi, but that's probably its fate."

I stared at the little bird, watching it flap its only wing. "Why was it born with just one wing, G-Pop?"

"Nature is like that sometimes."

"But I don't want it to die," Zandi said softly.

My eyes got watery. "Me neither. Can't we go up there and save it?"

Nana took a long, deep breath. "We're not having any more tree-climbing foolishness, Coop!"

"But we can't just let it die, Nana!"

"We could call the fire department," Zandi suggested. "They rescue cats, don't they?"

"A bird's not a cat," Nana replied. "Plus, I don't think they do that sort of thing anymore."

Tears streamed down Zandi's face.

G-Pop paced back and forth several times before he told us, "Dry your tears. I'll go get the ladder. We'll just have to make sure its parents are plenty busy elsewhere."

13

G-Pop CHECKED THAT the mockingbird parents were still nowhere to be found. Then he positioned the ladder under the nest, stepped up on the first rung, and stopped.

"What's wrong, Miles?" Nana asked.

"I'm going to need both hands to climb down, so where am I gonna put the little creature once I get ahold of it? Any ideas?"

I racked my brain and shouted, "I know! We can get some rope and tie it to the handles of a grocery bag, and you can put the bird inside and lower it down to us."

"That could work," G-Pop said. "Necessity truly is the mother of invention."

"Lemme guess. That means we invent things because we need them?"

"You're catching on, Coop."

It was quick and easy to assemble, and we finished in no time.

"Wish me luck," G-Pop said.

He was about to head up the ladder when my parents showed up.

"What's going on here?" Pops asked.

"One of the baby birds only has one wing and will never be able to fly," I told them.

"So I'm going up there to try and save it," G-Pop said.

"Otherwise, it'll die," Zandi added.

Mom shook her head in disbelief. "Haven't those birds caused enough trouble?"

Pops sighed. "C'mon, Dad, I don't want you falling too. This doesn't make sense."

I tapped his arm. "But what about the baby bird?"

Zandi gazed up at him and said, "We can't just leave it there."

Pops took a deep breath before he replied, "I'll go and try to get it . . . just hope those birds don't attack me too."

"Well, now is a good time," G-Pop told him, "because

the parents are off somewhere, probably getting food. But they could return anytime, so you'll have to hurry."

Mom shook her head again, but Pops gave her his don't-argue-with-me look, and as soon as G-Pop stepped off the ladder, Pops headed up.

Higher and higher he climbed. "Almost there!" he shouted.

Mom, Nana, and G-Pop held on to the bottom of the ladder to keep it from wobbling, and I waited nervously until Pops yelled, "Got it!"

Loudly, we cheered, and in no time, he carefully lowered the bag down to us.

Right away, we opened it to see. There it was—a baby mockingbird with just one wing.

14

POPS WAS HALFWAY down the ladder when the mom and pop mockingbirds returned. We heard squawking, and seconds later, their attack began. Angrily, they swooped at him, but Pops moved fast and made it to the ground safely. But the birds weren't done, and they came at us, forcing us to duck this way and that as we ran toward the house.

Once we got inside, Zandi reached into the bag, scooped up the baby bird, and put it on the wood floor.

Gently, I petted its feathers, and it looked at me and chirped. Then, cautiously, it took some steps.

"Where are we going to keep it?" I asked.

Zandi shrugged. "In a birdcage?"

That surprised G-Pop. "Thought you were dead set against birds being in cages, Miss Zandi?"

"I am mostly, but this is kind of a special case because it can't fly and it's little and we can't just let it roam around inside. If it does, someone might step on it."

"And bird poop will be everywhere," I said.

Pops, Mom, Nana, and G-Pop glanced at each other, and I guessed at what they were thinking.

"We can keep it, right?" I asked.

"Going to be kind of hard for you to take care of it with your arm still in a splint, Coop," Mom replied.

"I can keep it downstairs at my house," Zandi offered.

"But it's my bird," I argued.

"It doesn't just belong to you, Coop!"

"It was in my grandpop's tree, and if it weren't for him becoming a bird watcher, we probably never would have even known about it. So it belongs to me, and I'm gonna take it home."

"That's not fair!" Zandi fussed.

There was silence until G-Pop came to the rescue. "Time for a truce, you two . . . The bird can stay here. That way, it can belong to both of you. You'll be co-owners, so to speak. Does that sound like a deal?"

Zandi nodded and I did too. I figured if we kept fighting, we risked not being able to keep the bird at all.

Right then, the baby mockingbird took one hop and another and then hopped halfway across the room. "It'll never be able to fly," I told them, "but it sure can hop."

"Hop. That would be good name," Zandi suggested.

I smiled. "A bird named Hop. That's sorta cool."

Zandi picked up the bird from the floor and placed it in my cupped hand. As if expecting to be fed, the one-winged baby mockingbird cheeped and opened its mouth wide. "It seems hungry," I told them. "Wonder what we should feed it?"

"I'll look it up," Zandi said, and grabbed her cell phone.

Pops pulled out his, checked the time, and told me, "C'mon, Coop, we need to get going."

"Going where?"

"To the orthopedist's office for X-rays." So that's why he and mom had come.

"Will I finally be able to stop wearing the splint?"

"Not sure," he replied.

"But the bird . . . can't we do it another day?" I pleaded.

"Sorry, Coop, but we can't. It shouldn't take too long."

G-Pop rushed to the kitchen and returned holding a tin box with sides high enough to keep the bird from hopping out. "Our little friend will be just fine, Coop. Put it in here for now."

As I carefully placed Hop in the box, Zandi confidently informed me, "Don't worry, Coop. By the time you get back from the doctor, I will have learned everything we need to do to take good care of Hop."

15

WHEN HE CAME into the room with the X-rays, my doctor was smiling. "It's looking really good, Coop, almost completely healed."

The word *almost* stood out. "Almost," I repeated. "Does that mean I still have to wear the splint?"

He nodded. "But it won't be much longer," he promised.

"And once it's all better, I'll still be able to play basketball, right?"

"Your hand and arm are gonna be stiff for a while, so it'll take some time before it loosens up. Plus, the neurologist will have to say it's okay. Once all that happens, you'll be able to play ball again. What's your position?"

"Point guard."

"Are you pretty good?"

I grinned. "I'm not a star or anything, but I have some moves."

As we left the doctor's office, I felt like my finish line was finally within reach. I imagined myself back on the court and smiled. Then I thought about getting back to see Hop. And that's where we were heading when Mom got a text. "They need us to stop at the pet store to get a few things for the bird," she told Pops.

"Like what?" I asked.

"A birdcage, mealworms, a syringe, kitten food, and other stuff."

"Kitten food for a bird?" I asked.

"That's what it says, Coop."

"Wow, I guess we have a lot to learn about baby birds!"

16

As soon as I stepped inside G-Pop and Nana's, I asked two questions. "Where's Hop? And what's the kitten food for?"

Hop, I discovered, was still in the tin box, and the kitten food, Zandi explained, was part of a concoction we were going to make for the baby bird to eat. She had grabbed me by the arm and dragged me all the way to the kitchen before she noticed. "You still have your splint."

"Yeah, for another couple of weeks."

Zandi looked away, like she was thinking about something, then asked, "Doesn't it seem kinda weird?"

"What?"

"That your right arm's broken and the baby bird's right wing is missing."

I had to admit, it was a little strange, and after I'd let the weirdness of it swirl around inside my head for a while, I told her, "But there's a huge difference between me and Hop."

She made a goofy look. "You mean you're a boy and it's a bird? I just read we won't be able to tell if it's a boy or girl bird till it's older."

"No, that's not what I meant," I said. "It's that my arm's getting better, but Hop will always only have one wing."

"Yeah, you're right. Some things are forever."

I glanced into the box at Hop and told Zandi, "It really does stink that it'll never be able to fly like the others."

"But at least it won't die. Plus, it's in a safe place."

A safe place—that's what Mom and Pops always called the hospital where I'd been left. A safe place.

17

"How OFTEN DO we have to do this?" I asked Zandi after she had explained to all of us that we'd be feeding Hop through a syringe.

"The website said to feed fledglings every forty-five minutes to an hour, but only in the daytime," she replied.

"Phew. Glad it doesn't have to eat at night!" I said.

"Me too—and after a while, our bird should learn to feed itself."

The concoction Hop would be eating was a mixture of dry kitten food, birdseed, eggs, mealworms, fruit, and a bird vitamin. We followed the recipe and soaked the kitten food in water. Once it had softened, we mashed everything together and put the mixture in the syringe.

It sure didn't look like anything I'd ever want to eat! "You think it'll really like this stuff?"

"We're about to find out," G-Pop replied.

"I suppose just like hungry people, hungry birds aren't gonna be too picky," Pops joked.

"The video said it's extremely important not to over-feed, so just a little at a time until it stops opening its mouth for food," Zandi warned.

"Coop and Zandi, which of you wants to start?" G-Pop asked.

I was reluctant to try it first, and when Zandi's eyes met mine, I could see that she was too. "Maybe you should show us how, G-Pop," I told him.

Zandi agreed.

Everyone watched as G-Pop put the tip of the syringe to its beak. The baby bird opened widely, and G-Pop injected a tiny bit of the mixture and stopped. As if asking for more, the bird chirped several times.

"I suppose it likes it," Nana commented.

With G-Pop's help, I fed the bird next. "This is way too cool," I said.

Then Zandi took her turn until finally the small syringe was empty and Hop seemed full. As a reminder, we set the kitchen timer so we'd know when to feed it again, and afterward, we turned our attention to the bird-cage that would become its home.

According to Zandi, we needed to put grass and plants in the bottom of the cage along with a small bowl that the baby bird would hopefully think was a nest.

Nana rummaged around and found a small bamboo bowl, and then we gathered leaves, twigs, and other stuff from her garden. Once everything was ready, we scooped Hop out of the tin box and put it inside the cage.

"Sorry about having to put you in bird prison," I told it. "But we have to keep you safe because you only have one wing, so you'll never be able to fly."

I know it was impossible for the little bird to understand what I'd just said, but when it stared at me and chirped repeatedly, I wondered if somehow it did.

Zandi glanced at the wall clock, said, "Oops, it's my dinnertime," and in a flash was almost out the door. "Bye, everybody! See ya tomorrow!"

Dinnertime? We'd been so focused on Hop that none of us had even eaten lunch.

"Anyone else as hungry as I am?" Nana asked.

Of course we were.

She headed into the kitchen. "Hope spaghetti is okay?"

It was. And Mom, who likes to cook, offered to help her.

Soon the timer rang, alerting us to feed the bird again. This time Pops helped, and just like it had the first time, Hop ate greedily. "Your bird is an enthusiastic eater," Pops commented.

Afterward, like the lady at the pet store had advised, we gave it a few drops of water, but before we put the cage cover on, I told the baby mockingbird, "Good night, Hop."

"I'm kinda surprised," I told them.

"About what?" G-Pop asked.

"That we actually saved it."

"With three generations of Garnettes working together, there was no way for us to fail," Pops bragged.

Three generations of Garnettes? That made me feel good inside.

And later, after we'd gathered around the table and hungrily devoured the food, G-Pop got out his banjo and played.

18

EARLY THE NEXT morning, Pops dropped me off. Today it was just gonna be me and Nana since it was G-Pop's golf day and Zandi was somewhere with her mom.

After we fed Hop, we let the baby bird wander around on the kitchen floor for a while. When Nana invited me to go outside and help her in the garden, I told her no because I wanted to be alone with the bird, to have it all to myself for the very first time.

In order to get a really good look at the bird, I put Hop into the tin box. Carefully, I examined its beak, legs, and feet. It didn't seem to mind when I gently touched its tail and soft feathers or when I ran my finger over the place where its other wing should have been. Did it know that most birds have two wings—that most birds can fly?

When I stared into its tiny eyes, it chirped. I smiled and said, "Hey."

What exactly was it thinking? Was it wondering how it wound up with us instead of its bird parents? Right then, a thought popped into my mind. *Bird parents* and *birth parents* sounded almost the same, and all of a sudden I understood that even though Hop was a bird, and I wasn't, in one way we were exactly alike.

I scooped the bird into my hand again and explained, "Don't worry, I'm adopted too. You'll be okay."

I'd been feeling a lot of emotions lately, but now a new one snuck in and surprised me. I'd never felt needed, and now Hop, this little bird with just one wing, needed me. Being needed felt good.

I stared at Hop and promised, "I'll take good care of you and keep you safe."

19

Hop was beginning to chirp so much that I wondered if it could do more. I leaned in close and whistled a tune for the bird, hoping it might imitate me.

Nana smiled. "Did you know some people believe that human beings learned to make music and sing from listening to birds and that birdsong probably led to the creation of musical instruments?"

"So we have birds to thank for music?"

"Apparently," she replied.

Hop chirped again. "Wonder how long it'll be before it can actually sing like other mockingbirds."

"Don't know much about mockingbirds, Coop, except that they're songbirds, and songbirds sing."

"Hope it's soon, Nana."

"Me too, Coop," she said as she reached for her laptop. "The internet probably has some answers . . . Let's look it up."

Together we read through a bunch of articles. None told us exactly when baby mockingbirds begin to sing, but most of them did say that songbirds learn to sing from listening to their parents and other birds.

I glanced at Hop. "Do you think it can only learn to sing from other birds?"

"Not sure, Coop."

My ears tuned in to G-Pop's jazz, playing in the background, and I asked, "But they're called mockingbirds because they imitate. Can't it just learn from hearing our music?"

Nana shrugged.

"Let me get this straight—it'll never be able to fly, and it might never sing either?"

Nana patted my shoulder. "Let's not give up too easily, Coop. How about we play some videos of birds singing and see if Hop learns from them."

Nana turned off the jazz music and put her computer next to Hop's cage. We found some videos of mockingbirds singing, and soon the room was filled with nothing but birdsong, chirps, and tweets.

"A different kind of music, but beautiful music none-theless," she said.

My eyes were on Hop, hoping this would work, hoping Hop would soon join the bird chorus.

20

SINCE THE DAY we'd rescued their baby bird, the mom and pop mockingbirds had returned to the nest several times every day. As if they were searching for Hop, they pecked in and around the nest, squawking noisily, and I'd wondered more than once how they felt.

But today, for the first time, unless we had somehow missed seeing or hearing them, they hadn't come back to the nest even once. It was almost sundown.

"They must have finally given up," G-Pop remarked.

"So we probably don't have to worry about them attacking us again?" Zandi asked.

He nodded. "And if that's the case, it might be nice for

the little bird to be outside on the balcony in the fresh air," G-Pop advised.

I glanced at Hop, who was in the cage beside the computer, finishing up today's hour of listening to mockingbird songs. As soon as the music lesson ended, that's where we took it.

After we sat there awhile, Zandi suggested letting Hop out of the cage. "That way it can be a little free."

"Yeah, it's not like it can fly away."

We opened the cage door, and Zandi was about to reach in and pick it up when I told her, "Wait—mockingbirds are supposed to be really smart. Maybe it can find its way on its own."

Quietly and hopefully, we waited, and after what felt like a long time but probably wasn't, Hop found its way to the door and hopped out.

"See, Zandi, that's one smart bird."

Hop was happily hopping around when another young mockingbird landed on the ledge of the balcony. It was almost the same size as Hop. "Zandi," I whispered, and pointed. "You think it's one of Hop's brothers or sisters?"

Zandi nodded, and we stayed quiet and still so as not to scare the little bird away.

Soon the other bird began chirping, and Hop chirped right back.

Then, as their back-and-forth chirping continued, Hop began flapping its only wing while the other bird pranced along the balcony's ledge.

The two-winged mockingbird chirped once more before it took off. Zandi and I marveled as it flew, soaring through the air. It's what we'd been waiting and waiting to see, and all I could think was that they seemed so happy to see each other.

"Incredibly cool!" I exclaimed.

21

THE NEXT DAY, hoping the same little bird would come back to visit, we took Hop out on the balcony. As soon as we opened the cage's door, Hop quickly found its way out, and for more than an hour, we waited. As usual, a few birds flew by, and some even landed in the tree, but not a single mockingbird, as far as we could see.

"Maybe if we put the mealworm feeder on the balcony, they'll come," Zandi suggested.

But Nana said no and warned it might not just attract birds to her balcony, but other pests and critters too.

"But what can we do, then?" I asked. "Hop really likes being around other birds."

"How about one of those hummingbird feeders?" Nana proposed.

"It needs to be around songbirds, Nana, so it can learn to sing, remember?"

"And hummingbirds aren't exactly known for making music," Zandi added.

"This is true," she replied.

We'd been doing everything we could to take good care of the one-winged bird, feeding it and giving it water, keeping its cage clean, even making sure it had birdsong lessons, but Zandi and I had to admit, we'd never seen it happier than when it'd been chirping back and forth with the other little mockingbird. We decided there must be something we could do to make them come to visit and keep Hop from being lonely.

Once again, it was the internet to the rescue, and we found out there were many ways to make your backyard bird-friendly.

"This article says having a birdbath is a good way to lure birds," I told them.

Nana's face lit up. "Now, that's something I really could go for."

"And you were right, Nana."

"About what?"

"Sometimes bird feeders don't just attract birds. They attract other animals too, unless you have the kind that is specially made to keep pests away. Maybe we could buy one of those? It says mockingbirds really like something called suet, which is a mixture of stuff like seeds, fat, fruits, and nuts."

Zandi read the title of another article out loud. "'Using Your Backyard to Create a Bird Sanctuary.' What's a sanctuary?" she asked.

Nana answered, "A sanctuary is a safe place."

A safe place—there were those words again. Now I'd learned there was another word for it too, a sanctuary. "Sanctuary," I whispered, then announced, "That's exactly what we're going to make, a bird sanctuary." I grabbed a pen and paper to start the list.

A birdbath, of course, was number one, and the kind that was recommended had a fountain. Nana, who'd been wanting a fountain in her garden for a very long time, was all smiles. We found a place not far away on Pico Boulevard that had some, and after we fed Hop, that's where we headed. Luckily, G-Pop had a four-seater pickup truck.

22

WHILE THE HANDYMAN installed the birdbath fountain, Zandi and I, with a little help from G-Pop, were assembling two birdhouses from kits we'd bought. Nana was busily planting sunflowers and different kinds of daisies that she'd learned were guaranteed to attract songbirds.

As we worked, Zandi filled us in on some brand-new bird facts. "Did you know that just like us, birds need to take baths to keep their feathers clean?"

That made perfect sense, we all agreed.

"And," she continued, "for some reason, taking baths makes them better at flying."

I laughed. "I guess it's harder to fly with dirty wings."

"Yeah, because dirt on the feathers would make them weigh more," Zandi added.

G-Pop gazed up to where the now-empty nest was. "Having that pair of mockingbirds build their nest in our tree has opened up a whole new world for you two, hasn't it?"

"It sure has," Zandi replied. "With everything I'm learning, I could practically be an ornithologist."

She glanced at me like she didn't expect me to know that word, but because I'd started doing a little bird research of my own, I knew exactly what an ornithologist was. "You mean a bird expert." And when Zandi gave me a look that told me I'd surprised her, I, Coop Garnette, grinned.

Soon the handyman finished hooking up the birdbath fountain, and when he turned it on, the water whooshed, gurgled, and spouted.

Right away, I searched the sky, looking for birds. "How long do you think it'll be before they start coming to the birdbath?"

"They'll come when they come," Nana replied, "the same way bees and butterflies show up in my garden."

"You think Hop's old enough to take a bath?" Zandi asked.

G-Pop nodded. "It certainly has every right to be our first customer."

Zandi and I rushed upstairs and got the birdcage. There wasn't that much water in the fountain, but before we slid Hop into the bath, I needed to be sure about something. "It won't drown, will it?"

"In so little water, I doubt it," G-Pop replied.

As soon as Hop hit the water, the little bird started having fun, splishing and splashing, happily flapping its one wing in the sparkling water.

Everyone, including the handyman, was smiling, and right then I knew that making the bird sanctuary had been a very good idea.

Now, if we could just attract some other songbirds so that Hop could learn to sing.

23

BY THE END of the week, we were finished making our sanctuary. Bird feeders that other animals would have a hard time raiding were set up, and the birdhouses Zandi and I had made were hung. Nana's new flowers added even more colors to her garden, and the hummingbird feeder she'd wished for was hanging on the balcony and filled with nectar.

Earlier, before G-Pop left to play golf, he surprised us with a hand-painted sign that read, **Coop and Zandi's Bird Sanctuary.**

Once the sign was up, I proclaimed, "We did it!" And then, because we knew some birds are afraid of people and might not come with us around, we headed back inside.

Like we did nearly every day, we brought Hop out to the balcony and let it out of the cage to explore. While the little bird wandered around, Zandi and I staked out the sanctuary with our binoculars.

I was wishing for a way to make lots of birds magically appear when Zandi elbowed me. "Coop, there's a bird at one of the bird feeders!"

Already? I zoomed in and there it was, a small gray bird with a black crest on its head. The same kind of bird had probably flown past me hundreds of times, but I'd never paid attention. "Wonder what kind it is?" I asked.

Zandi shrugged. "There are more than ten thousand species of birds. It'd be practically impossible for anyone to know them all."

Minutes later, when a bird landed on the ledge of the balcony, I said, "Now, that's an easy one. It's a white dove." Trying to show off, I added, "Doves are smaller and thinner than pigeons."

For a while, the dove cooed softly, and then it flew away.

At first, when I heard a bird singing, I thought maybe I was imagining things—but I wasn't.

The bird that was perched in the tree wasn't just any bird—it was a full-grown mockingbird, and it seemed kind of familiar. "You think it's Hop's mom or pop?" I asked Zandi.

"Maybe. I read that mockingbirds are territorial and usually stay in the same neighborhood."

I hadn't thought about that when I'd suggested the bird sanctuary. If there was one thing I wasn't in the mood for, it was another bird attack. I glanced down at Hop. Did the bird that was perched in the tree know it was here? Was that why it had come? Had it been sent as a decoy while its mate waited quietly somewhere, preparing for the ambush? Worried, I asked Zandi, "Do you think they're still mad at us?"

"Maybe. Supposedly they have good memories."

The bird kept on singing.

"But those birds never sang," I reminded her, "so maybe it's a different bird."

"Sometimes they don't sing when they're taking care of their baby birds," she replied.

Then, as if it knew we were watching, the bird turned our way and began to spread its tail and raise and lower its wings while it sang.

Nana, who'd joined us on the balcony, declared, "It's putting on quite a show, isn't it? Now, that's what I call an entertainer."

G-Pop's claim that mockingbirds know a lot of music must have been true because this bird sang on and on, and as it did, every now and then, Hop chirped.

But because I was afraid it might be a trap, I didn't really enjoy the performance. Anticipating another double-team attack, I remained on the lookout.

24

THE TIME HAD come to go back to the orthopedic doctor, and I hoped my fiasco was finally coming to an end. I nervously waited for the X-ray results, and when the doctor opened the door, his smiling face told me my wish had been granted. "Everything healed perfectly," he said proudly.

"No more splint?" I asked.

He patted my shoulder. "No more splint, Coop. And remember, you told me you'd stay out of trees, right?"

"I promise."

After he showed me some exercises to do, I asked, "So I can play ball now, right? Last week the neurologist said I could if you said it's okay."

"Sure, Coop. You can play ball. But you'll have to take it slow at first."

"I will. Thanks, Doc."

As we left, I joked with Mom, "Well, at least the Coop-Garnette-fell-out-of-a tree story had a happy ending."

She glanced over at me and smiled. "Yes, it did, Coop . . . yes, it did."

25

It was the night that the Los Angeles Philharmonic invited a few talented kids to perform with them. My mom and I went every year.

Mom's eyes lit up when she talked about the event. "Each one is an absolutely amazing young musician."

Absolutely amazing young musician—those weren't words anyone was ever going to use to describe Coop Garnette.

As if not being the slightest bit musical wasn't enough, coming from a musical family created another problem. Usually, whenever I first met my pops' and mom's musician friends, they always *assumed* that I inherited their musical talent. They grinned from ear to ear as if it was my destiny to become one of them, the music people.

The Fourth of July Spectacular at the Hollywood Bowl was one thing, but being forced to sit for hours listening to musical-genius kids, secretly wishing I could be like them, was something else.

"I don't wanna go," I told my mom. "Besides, I'm no good at music."

"But a person doesn't have to be good at music to enjoy it, Coop." She paused. "Do you enjoy music?"

"Yeah, I do."

"Then that's good enough."

"Is it?" I blurted out. "Don't you ever wish you'd gotten one of those musical-genius kids instead of me?"

The look on her face let me know I'd hurt her feelings, and I wished I could take it back. But I'd already said it, so I couldn't. There were tears in her eyes when she walked over to me, put her arms around me, and softly said, "Of course not, Coop." Her hugging made me feel good, so I let it last for a while. "I'd never thought about it, but us being all about music is hard for you, isn't it?"

Since I was in a being-honest mood, I replied, "Yeah,

it kinda is. And your music friends who don't know I'm adopted always expect me to be good at it."

"Sorry," she said, and hugged me even more tightly. "For the record, Coop Garnette, even if you hated music, I'd still love you, and I'll always be glad we chose you and that somehow you chose us."

"I chose you?" I'd never heard her say that before, and I was a little confused. "But I was just a baby. How could I choose you?"

"Some choices are made by the heart and spirit. And some things, it seems, are just meant to be."

I kind of understood what she was saying. "Oh."

We stopped hugging. "If you don't want to go, I'll understand. I can drop you off at your nana's."

I took a minute to decide. "No, that's okay. But do I have to dress fancy?"

My mom, Willow Garnette, chuckled and nodded.

Fancy clothes or not, getting dressed was easy again because I could finally use both arms, and that felt good.

BEFORE THE CONCERT started, I was standing with Mom when this lady rushed over to us. Mom hugged her, then introduced us.

"Coop, this is Lilly. She used to play violin in the orchestra with your pops."

Lilly smiled. "Nice to meet you, Coop."

"Nice to meet you too," I told her.

And then it began. "How fantastic it must be to be born into such a gifted musical family. I'm sure you inherited lots of talent and are quite the musician. What instruments do you play, Coop?" Lilly asked.

Was this ever going to end? I looked at Mom as if to say, *See what I mean?* I could tell she was getting ready to come to my rescue, but before my mom could save me, I, Coop Garnette, decided to save myself.

"I don't play any instruments, and I didn't inherit any talent from them because I'm adopted," I said.

Lilly looked extremely embarrassed and replied, "Oh."

Then, in no time flat, she said goodbye and rushed off.

I waited for Mom's lecture about being impolite, but probably because of the talk we'd had earlier, it never came.

And every now and then during the concert, I still wished I was one of the absolutely amazing young musicians onstage with the orchestra—but mostly I just enjoyed the music.

26

BEFORE THE FIASCO, I'd been the best point guard on my basketball team, the Meteors. I knew I was nowhere near ready for a return to the court, but one of the other players, Mason, was having a birthday party and I'd been invited.

"Coop Garnette returns!" Mason announced when I made my entrance to the backyard patio. Music was playing and the smoker was going, meaning barbecue was on its way.

As my team members crowded around me, they were all smiles. We butted knuckles and it felt great that they were so happy to see me. Mason's mom kissed my forehead, and our coach, Mr. Andrews, a.k.a. Mason's father, gave me a shoulder hug.

Josiah, our forward, who's into poetry, proclaimed, "Even crashing to the ground . . . can't keep one of the Meteors down!" Applause and cheers followed.

"You are one lucky dude, Coop," another player commented as we waited in line for food. He eyed the scar on my forehead. "A coma . . . were you terrified? I know I woulda been."

As soon as I replied, "Not really," I realized I was lying, and from the look he gave me, I wondered if he did too. It was scary thinking about how close I'd come to never waking up again, and some things, like my coordination, still weren't quite the same. Fortunately my brain hadn't felt foggy for a while, but I worried whether I'd still be good at math when school started. My eyes darted around at my friends. Did I seem different to them now? I hoped not. Was I, like the doctors kept promising, going to be 100 percent Coop Garnette again? I hoped so.

Later, as we sat around the table, laughing, clowning, and eating, Nelson, our center, interrupted our fun. "We heard you adopted a bird, Coop."

When I'm around people who know I'm adopted and someone says that word, sometimes a strange quiet descends. Today was no different. Everyone seemed embarrassed and the whole table looked at Nelson like he'd just dumped on me. When someone finally elbowed him, he got that *oops* look.

I wanted to tell him that it was okay to say the word *adopt* in front of me—unless you were saying it like it was a bad thing. I also wanted to let them know that I wasn't ashamed to be adopted, but it bothered me when people thought that I was. And though I was glad adoption existed, there were many times when I wished the word didn't.

I wanted to say all that stuff, but it seemed too complicated to explain, so instead I just looked at him and replied, "Yeah, I adopted a mockingbird. It was born with just one wing, so it'll never fly. But it's smart and can still hop and do other stuff, and it probably would have died if we hadn't rescued it."

"So the bird's lucky like you, huh, Coop?" Mason said.

I shrugged and replied, "I suppose."

In bed that night, I stared at the ceiling. The fiasco had eaten up most of my summer break, and being around my friends again had reminded me that I'd lost out on a whole summer of fun with them.

Because I was alive and getting better, people kept

reminding me of how lucky I'd been. But if I was truly lucky, would I have had the accident in the first place? Right then I wondered exactly how much luck a person gets. Maybe some people get more luck than others. There were times when it seemed that way. Did luck, like a car out of gas, ever run out? And if so, had I used up all of mine?

27

MONDAY MORNING, AS we drove to G-Pop and Nana's, I was thinking that I really wanted to be heading somewhere else. And that somewhere else was practicing b-ball with the Meteors. They'd asked me to come to the gym to watch, but I wanted to play, not just warm the bench, so I'd said no. I ran my fingers over the scar on my arm from the surgery. At home, I'd tried dribbling, but my wrist was stiff, so my ball-handling skills were a joke. Afterward my whole arm was sore, and I doubted I'd ever be good on the court again.

But at least the bird sanctuary was bustling. Like people telling each other about a good restaurant, the birds must have been spreading the word, because the sanctuary was becoming a very popular place. The birdbath was always in demand, with Nana's hummingbird feeder a close second. The birdhouses, however, remained vacant.

"Maybe we should put a For Rent sign on them," G-Pop had joked.

That day, after we fed Hop, Zandi put the little bird back in the cage and brought it out to the balcony for fresh air, like we did almost every day. Later, after we'd finished up in the sanctuary, we'd come back and let it out to explore. But to keep our bird safe from predators, whenever it was alone, we always made sure Hop was safe inside the cage. G-Pop was working on something in the garage, and Nana was busy doing laundry.

Zandi and I were cleaning the bird feeders in the sanctuary when we noticed two hawks circling above, high in the sky. "Hawks mate for life," Zandi said. "And there's even one called a Cooper's hawk," she added.

I cracked up laughing. "A Cooper's hawk? No way."

"Yep," Zandi said, and she showed me some pictures of Cooper's hawks on her phone.

I gazed up at the hawks, which seemed to be floating on air. To get a better look at them, I rushed inside to get my binoculars. While I was there, one of them landed on the ledge of the balcony. It looked like a Cooper's hawk, but I needed to get closer to be certain. As I cautiously made my approach, the hawk watched me for a moment, then flapped away and perched nearby on a branch in the tree.

Right then, I glanced at Hop's cage, which was still on the balcony where Zandi had put it earlier, but the little bird wasn't inside and the cage door was open, which was strange. I looked around until I finally saw Hop. "How'd you get out of your cage?" I asked.

I was heading for Hop when the hawk suddenly swooped in and beat me to it.

"Stop!" I yelled.

With its clawed feet, the hawk picked up Hop!

"Let it go!" I hollered, and whacked at the hawk with my hand.

Luckily, it dropped the baby bird on the balcony. I expected the hawk to fly away, but it wasn't ready to give up. It turned and swooped for Hop again. Except this time I outmaneuvered it. "Go away!" I screamed as I dived to shield the little bird with my body, accidentally falling on it.

By the time Zandi, Nana, and G-Pop showed up, I was sitting cross-legged on the balcony, holding Hop.

"What's all the commotion?" G-Pop asked.

I stared at the limp bird in my hands and whimpered, "I think Hop's dead."

28

ALL EYES WERE on the lifeless little bird.

G-Pop let out a long sigh and asked, "What happened, Coop?"

"A hawk went after it."

G-Pop shook his head and muttered, "A hawk . . . who'da thought."

The truth was, I didn't know if Hop had died from when the hawk grabbed it or if I had crushed the small bird when I'd landed on top of it. But I did know there was only one word to describe the way Coop Garnette felt—miserable.

Then, all of a sudden, like a bolt of lightning, it hit me.

Zandi must have left the cage door open, and if she hadn't, Hop would've been safe and still alive.

I glared at her. "I can't believe you left the cage door open! This is all your fault!"

"I thought I closed it," Zandi said, and she started to cry.

"You might've thought it, but you didn't do it!" I hollered.

Nana told me to calm down, but I couldn't.

"I'm sorry! I'm sorry! I'm sorry!" Zandi was crying harder, and when she headed downstairs, Nana was right behind her.

Gently, I held Hop to my chest, and as I embraced the bird, I could swear I felt it move!

I examined it closely and waited hopefully, but nothing happened. So much for wishful thinking.

G-Pop came and settled on the floor beside me. Quietly we sat, until I turned to him and sadly said, "It never even got a chance to sing."

He put his arm around my shoulder and pulled me close.

29

G-Pop BROUGHT ME the tin box we'd put Hop in that day we'd rescued it. "Put your bird in here, Coop. We'll bury it later."

As I placed the limp bird in the box, I remembered promising to take good care of it and keep it safe. Both promises had been broken. "Sorry," I whispered to the little bird, and tears were in my eyes when I asked G-Pop, "Do you think making the bird sanctuary is what made those hawks come?"

"There's no way to know if that's what brought the hawks here. Some, like Cooper's hawks, are native to the area. I've seen them around now and then."

"That's the other thing that stinks, it was a *Cooper's* hawk."

"An unlucky coincidence, Coop," G-Pop replied.

I had another question. "Was it all just a waste of time?"

"What?"

"Saving a baby bird, feeding it, trying to teach it to sing, when it was going to wind up dying anyway."

"No, I don't think it was a waste of time."

"I wish those mockingbirds had never built their nest in that tree. Then I wouldn't have—"

"Gotten hurt?"

"Yeah, that too . . . but mostly, I wouldn't be sad right now because . . . I dunno." I shrugged.

"Because you loved the little bird?" he asked.

I hadn't thought about that word, *love*, but I knew he was right. "Yeah . . . I suppose."

"Love is never a waste of time, Coop."

30

G-Pop HAD GONE searching for the box's lid when I thought I saw Hop's wing move. But I decided my brain was probably imagining things and acting a little wonky again. I peered down into the sanctuary, where Nana and Zandi were sitting side by side on a bench in the garden. Zandi should have made sure the cage door was closed. Even if she said sorry a million times, it would never be enough. I started to cry.

"Found it!" G-Pop shouted, and then he reappeared on the balcony.

We were standing over the table and G-Pop was about to put the lid on Hop's box when he asked, "Did you see that, Coop? I think the bird took a breath."

I wiped my tears. "What? I thought I saw it move a little while ago, but I figured my mind was playing tricks on me."

Together we watched and were amazed to see Hop open and shut its beak, and then give its wing a little shake.

It wasn't wishful thinking after all! "It's alive," I yelled and ran over to edge of the balcony. "Nana! Zandi! Come quick! Hop is alive."

"Just barely," G-Pop warned. "We've got to get it to the animal hospital. Hurry!"

31

While G-Pop drove, Nana called ahead to a local veterinarian, who said they didn't take care of birds but gave her the name of an avian veterinarian who wasn't too far away. When Nana called them, they told her to get there as fast as we could.

I held the box, and my eyes stayed glued on Hop, watching. Now and then it took a slow breath, then a bunch of quick ones, then nothing.

"It's like it's trying really hard to stay alive," Zandi said.

I knew she was trying to get me to talk, but it was her fault that Hop was barely hanging on, so I ignored her.

"Sorry, Coop," Zandi whispered.

"Okay," I replied, but not in a friendly way.

We hadn't been driving too long, but in the way it does when you're in a hurry, it felt like forever. I glanced at the truck's GPS navigation screen. "We'll be there in ten minutes," I told Hop. "Don't die."

"Slow down, Miles," Nana warned each time G-Pop sped up, and then we caught three red lights in a row—the longest red lights in the history of the universe.

Finally, we got there. The sign said AVIAN VETERINARIAN/PET HOSPITAL. Before we even came to a stop, I was halfway out of the truck.

"Slow down, Coop," Nana warned.

But how could I?

Convinced that the help my bird needed was on the other side of that door, I bolted and hoped that Hop's fiasco was going to end up like mine—some kind of miracle.

32

THERE WERE A few people with caged birds sitting in the waiting room.

"May I help you?" a woman behind the counter asked.

I held out the tin box so she could see Hop. "This is an emergency situation! It's dying!"

Soon G-Pop, Nana, and Zandi arrived.

The receptionist made a call. "The doctor can see you now," she said, but when all four of us headed to the door, she told us, "I'm sorry, but you can't all go in at once, only two at a time."

Moments later, G-Pop and I were buzzed through the door and led to a room where the veterinarian was waiting.

"I'm Dr. Bloom," she said as she put gloves on.

"Pleased to meet you, Dr. Bloom. I'm Miles Garnette, and this is my grandson, Coop."

Her eyes darted from G-Pop to me. "The family resemblance is remarkable."

G-Pop gently touched my shoulder. "That's what people say."

This had always been one of those strangely weird things—that even though G-Pop and I weren't related by blood, we actually did look alike. At times like this, I began wondering what my birth parents looked like, and who I resembled.

But as soon as the bird doctor started examining Hop, all other thoughts vanished.

"It's a northern mockingbird" was the first thing out of the doctor's mouth.

"We know," I said.

"And it only has one wing" was the next thing she told us.

"Born that way," G-Pop informed her.

The next thing she said was "It's not dead," and I asked myself, *Is she ever going to tell us something we don't already know?*

But then she started questioning us. "Did it fall from a tree?"

"No," I replied, and explained about the hawk grabbing it and dropping it.

"And was that when you found it?"

"No, we discovered it only had one wing when it was still in the nest, and we rescued it then. Otherwise, it would have died." Proudly, I rattled off all the things we had done for the little bird, including feeding it, trying to teach it to sing, and creating the backyard bird sanctuary. "Usually we keep it in a cage so it's safe, but today"—I sighed—"someone forgot to close the cage door and it got out . . . and that was when the hawk got it."

"So you keep it caged as a pet?"

I nodded.

That was when she got a strange look on her face and glanced at G-Pop.

"Is it going to die?" I asked her.

"Well, first, I have to tell you that what you've done to help this bird and making the sanctuary is commendable. These days, wild birds need all the help they can get."

Wild? I didn't really consider Hop to be wild. "Thank you," I said proudly.

"The second thing you should know is that this young mockingbird is a he."

"Oh . . . a he." I chuckled. "His name is Hop."

"Well, Coop, Hop is what we call stunned. Sometimes it happens when a bird flies into a window. In Hop's case, it's probably a result of the fall. Some birds recover completely, but others don't. We'll keep him overnight, give supportive care, and hope for the best."

"I fell out of a tree and now I'm practically as good as new," I informed her. "So he'll probably be okay too."

She smiled.

"Can I stay with him overnight?"

"I'm afraid that won't be possible."

"But what if he dies?" I asked. "I don't want him to be alone."

"We'll do our best," Dr. Bloom said, and G-Pop patted my shoulder.

I took another look at Hop. "See ya," I said. "Hang in there, little dude."

We started to leave, and the vet stopped G-Pop. "Can I speak to you alone, Mr. Garnette?" she asked.

"Of course," he replied, then told me, "You can go up front with your nana and Zandi, Coop."

I hovered outside the door to eavesdrop, but they were speaking so quietly I couldn't make out what they were saying, so I headed to the waiting room.

33

"THE DOCTOR SAYS he might be okay," I told Nana and Zandi.

"He?" they both asked.

"Yeah, he," I replied, then explained everything the bird doctor had told us.

When G-Pop joined us in the waiting room, he wasn't smiling.

"What'd she say?" I asked him.

My grandfather stared into my eyes. "We'll talk later, Coop."

The words *talk later* and the look on his face could only mean one thing—bad news.

As we walked outside, I couldn't help myself. I had to ask, "He's gonna die, huh?"

"Too soon to tell, Coop."

"Well, if he's gonna die, I'm not leaving him here. Let's just take him home."

"He has a point, Miles," Nana said.

"It's not that." G-Pop paused. "She actually thinks the little bird has a fighting chance."

"Then why won't you tell me?"

G-Pop sighed. "All right, Coop. Even if the bird survives, you probably can't keep him, because northern mockingbirds can't be kept as caged pets!"

"Says who?" Zandi asked.

"The federal government. They're a protected species."

"But he only has one wing, so he has to be in a cage, or it'll happen again," I said.

G-Pop spoke up. "The vet thinks he should be in a bird rehabilitation center. She has a friend who takes in sick and injured birds . . . and he wouldn't be alone."

I shook my head. "I'm not giving him away to strangers! It's just one bird. The government doesn't care about just one bird. Plus, he's not alone. He has us. We can take care of him."

"Yeah, we can," Zandi said.

G-Pop sighed again. "He'd be safe there."

"But he was safe with us until . . ." I glanced over at Zandi. "From now on, *I'll* protect him." And then I blurted out what I was most afraid of. "Besides, he still might die! And if he does, all this stuff we're talking about won't even matter!"

Everything got quiet.

And when G-Pop walked away to make a call, Zandi leaned toward me and whispered, "They can't actually make us give him away, can they?"

I shrugged. "I dunno."

I stared at the vet's office. If it really was a law, they probably could force us. But would they? That was something else altogether.

"I'm prepared to do whatever it takes to keep the bird," I told her.

Zandi nodded. "Yeah, whatever it takes."

34

POPS WAS WAITING outside when we got to my house. And from the look on his face, I guessed that the phone call G-Pop had made was to my dad, and that he had already filled him in. Were they about to join forces and try to persuade me to give up my bird?

I flashed back to that day in the tree when the birds, by double-teaming me, had sent me to my defeat. If that's what G-Pop and Pops were scheming, at least this time I'd be expecting it, and according to Coach Andrews, anticipating your opponent's moves usually gives you an advantage and sometimes leads to victory. If Hop did survive, this was one battle Coop Garnette didn't want to lose.

What I needed was time—time to come up with some smooth moves of my own.

"See ya, Coop," G-Pop said.

"Let's hope he'll be okay," Nana added.

Zandi gave me a thumbs-up and I returned it, then waved to them as they drove off.

Today, Pops was wearing orange plaid pants, a turquoise tee with a huge red bulldog on the front, and neon-green Vans. His colorful outfits usually amused me, but not right now. Nothing could amuse me today. His mouth was smiling but his eyes weren't, which confirmed my suspicions.

"G-Pop told you, huh?"

He nodded. "How 'bout we take a walk to the park?"

"Not if you're gonna try to convince me to give the bird away. We should at least wait till we know if he's gonna live or die, right? Otherwise, it's a waste of time."

From the look on his face, I knew I'd scored some points, and since the ball was in my court, I decided to make some more. "And it's just one little bird, Pops. Besides, you can't just save something and start to care about it and then give it away. You wouldn't give me away, would you?"

"Of course not, Coop . . . but you're not a bird, so it's a huge difference."

"Not to me, it isn't. Besides, he needs me."

Pops got that I-feel-sorry-for-you-bro look again, the one he'd had when I was in the hospital. He gave me a shoulder hug and then did what he often does when he can't figure out what to say next—he changed the subject. "It's been a hard day, hasn't it, Coop? How about we shoot some hoops at the park? Maybe some b-ball will take your mind off things for a while and make you feel better."

I wanted to tell him that just the other day, when I'd gone down to the park to see what I could do, I'd been clumsy dribbling the ball and I couldn't even make a shot from the free-throw line. I left the court with my head down, feeling like a failure. No, shooting hoops was definitely not going to make me feel better, especially today.

But Pops looked at me pitifully and said, "Please?"

So I said, "Okay."

When he opened the garage to get the ball, Mom's car was gone. "Where's Mom?" I asked.

"She went to get stuff to make lasagna," he replied.

Lasagna, my favorite.

Quietly we strolled to the park, but when some birds

landed nearby, chirping and chattering, I thought about Hop and broke the silence. "I hope he doesn't die, Pops."

"He?"

"Yeah, Hop's a he. And I want him to live."

"So do I, Coop." He paused. "You really like birds, don't you?"

"Yeah, they're fascinating."

Pops smiled.

"Don't you think it's a stupid law? I bet there are a gazillion mockingbirds."

"Maybe there are now, but according to what I just read online, their singing ability made them very common pets, and by the early 1900s they were almost extinct. Now they're protected by federal law and also some kind of treaty act and can't be kept captive."

I sighed. "Hop's not a captive, we're keeping him safe. Because he's special, with just one wing. He *has* to be in a cage."

"It's still against the law."

Normally when a person is given two choices, they don't both stink, but in this case, they did. "So I either break the law or let Hop out of the cage and he dies?"

Pops patted my shoulder. "There is a third choice, Coop. The vet has a friend who's a wildlife rehabilitator and takes in injured birds. She even has a good-sized aviary on her property where he could stay. And several of her birds only have one wing . . . mostly from being injured."

"So they'll never fly either?"

"Precisely. And . . . the vet thought if Hop does recover, he might be happier living there with the other birds. He wouldn't have to be caged up, and he'd be in a safe place."

A safe place. Those words again.

I was on the verge of tears, but luckily we'd reached the park and no one was on the court. Pops dribbled and passed me the ball.

From the free-throw line, I eyed the hoop, bounced the ball a few times, then shot with my right hand. Total air ball. And I still felt a pang in my wrist.

Pops grabbed the ball and passed it to me again. "This time, try shooting with your left hand."

My left hand? I'd gotten pretty good at doing some things with it, but shooting hoops felt awkward at first.

On my third try, the ball at least hit the rim.

"That's it, Coop!" Pops said as he passed me the ball again.

Finally, on my sixth try, the sound of the ball as it swished through the net was sweet. Pops cheered, and I pictured myself back on the court with the Meteors, now possessing a rare skill—a righty who could shoot left-handed.

We played until I got tired, and as we walked home, my arm ached a little. I thought about Hop and wondered how much it would hurt to let him go to be with the other birds.

Probably a lot.

35

BEFORE WE EVEN got inside the house, I smelled the lasagna cooking and my mouth started watering.

"I made lasagna, your favorite," Mom said. "It'll be ready in a while."

I wasn't as hungry as usual, but I told her, "Thanks, Mom," and headed to my cave.

I plopped on the bed, stared at the ceiling, and tried my hardest to squeeze everything out of my brain. I really didn't want to think, especially about Hop, but that didn't last long. I pictured my little bird and hoped he'd be okay.

After a while I started wishing G-Pop hadn't taught me about coins having two sides, because I, Coop Garnette, really only wanted to see the side where I got to keep Hop and someday hear him sing. I didn't want to look at the other side, where Hop got to be with other birds and be kind of free.

He seemed happy with me and Zandi and the rest of the Garnettes, and he always chirped when he first saw me. We'd become his family, hadn't we? Just like the Garnettes had become mine. Would this bird lady and the other birds love him better than we did? I doubted it. Plus, I had a feeling that someday Hop was going to sing, and I wanted to hear those songs.

So right now, keeping Hop was the only side of the coin I was going to look at—and even though I knew it wasn't true, I imagined that the other side of the coin was blank.

36

ONE WAY TO buy yourself more time is to get up early, so the next morning, that's what I did. Mom and Pops were still sleeping when I quietly got dressed, grabbed my hidden stash of birthday money, and snuck out of the house. I, Coop Garnette, needed as much time with Hop as I could possibly get. I remembered from yesterday that the sign at the vet's said they open at 8:00 a.m. It was only seven, but it was kind of far away, which meant I needed to walk fast. I glanced at my watch, picked up my pace, and took long strides.

As parents go, Mom and Pops Garnette were pretty smart, and I figured that it would take them less than sixty seconds to figure out where I was headed. I only hoped that the way I'd put the pillows under my blankets would convince them I was still fast asleep and give me even more of a head start.

Because I'd never done anything like this before, I felt a little uneasy. And I hoped that when I explained it to them later, they'd understand. Besides, it wasn't like I was running away or anything. If Hop was okay, I just wanted this chance to hang out with him—a chance I wasn't sure they'd give me.

As planned, I got there just as they were opening. So far, so good.

Today, the waiting room was empty. "My name's Coop Garnette, and my bird's name is Hop, and I came to see him," I told the receptionist at the desk.

By the smile she flashed, I could tell she remembered me. "The doctor just got here. Let me check for you."

Before I sat down, I patted the wad of bills in my back pocket. "Please let him be all better," I whispered. Nervously, I tapped my feet as I waited, and my patience started to fade.

When the receptionist finally came back, before she had a chance to even open her mouth, I asked, "Is my bird okay?"

"The doctor will be able to talk with you in a few minutes," she replied. "You're not all by yourself, are you? Is your grandfather outside?"

Hmm? She was asking about G-Pop and acting like she wanted to make sure I wasn't alone. Was this code for "bad news is about to be delivered"?

"He's coming in a little while," I told her as I approached her desk. I wanted to be close enough to get a really good look at her eyes when I asked my next question. "I have a right to know. Is my bird dead?"

She was about to answer me when Dr. Bloom, the bird vet, stuck her head into the waiting room. "Hi, Coop. Where's your grandfather today?"

The receptionist answered for me. "He should be here soon."

As Dr. Bloom ushered me through the door, her happy face let the cat out of the bag. "I'm pleased to tell you that your bird, Hop, has made a complete recovery."

I know I shouldn't have, but I let out a very loud hoot, then hollered, "Thank you! Thank you! Thank you!"

37

DR. BLOOM LED me to a room lined with birdcages, and I practically flew to the one where Hop was.

When my little bird looked up at me and chirped, I decided I'd done the right thing by coming here like this. "Hey, little dude," I said. He looked the same as ever, and that made me really happy.

"Can I take him now?" I asked the vet. "I have the money to pay you."

She got that confused look. "Didn't your grandfather talk to you about mockingbirds?"

"Yes, he told me there's a law against keeping them as pets. And that your friend has an aviary where Hop will be safe." I stared into her eyes and told her the truth. "But

I just want to spend a little more time alone with him for one more day, to kind of say goodbye."

"And then you'll bring him to my friend's aviary?"

I nodded.

"I understand, Coop . . . I understand," she said. "Giving up your bird is a difficult decision, but there are reasons for laws like these." She patted my shoulder.

"So I can take him, right?"

She replied yes and took a card out of her pocket. "I was going to give this to your grandfather today. It's the contact information for the wildlife rehabilitator. It's not too far, out by the beach. I'm sure Hop will be happy there. I called her yesterday, and she'll be expecting you."

I took the card and, without even looking at it, put it in my pocket. Then I pulled out the wad of bills and offered them to her. "Thank you for saving him."

She smiled and replied, "Keep your money. There's no charge."

"How come?"

"Not only did you save the bird, Coop, you helped set up your own bird sanctuary. As a bird lover, I think you've already repaid your debt. Birds are very special, aren't they?"

"Yeah, they are."

She patted my shoulder again, and when I asked if she

still had the tin box so I could take Hop home, she offered to loan me a spare birdcage instead.

At the front door, I told her, "My grandfather should be here any minute. I'll wait outside." I didn't feel good about lying, but my mission had been to get to spend at least one more day with Hop, and that mission, it appeared, was about to be accomplished.

The bird vet and the lady at the front desk smiled at me and waved goodbye, and when I smiled back, it felt like I'd pulled a fast one.

I carried the cage outside, and to make them think I was waiting for G-Pop to come, I stood there for a while. Then, once I was pretty sure they weren't watching, Coop Garnette and his bird, Hop, made their escape.

38

By the time I turned the corner at the end of the block, I realized that other than getting the vet to let me have the bird, I really didn't have a plan. What the heck was I doing? Where was I going to go?

By now, Mom and Pops had probably discovered that I was missing. Without a doubt they'd called G-Pop and Nana, and something told me that between the four of them, my whereabouts were about to be pinpointed, so I knew I had to keep moving.

I was scoping out the neighborhood when the answer to my question showed up. I'd reached a bus stop at the same time as a bus, and when it stopped to let a passenger off, without thinking I climbed aboard.

"Okay if I bring my bird?" I asked the bus driver.

"As long as it's in a cage. And you have to keep it on your lap," she replied.

"Where we going, anyway?" I asked as I paid the fare.

"Venice Beach is the end of the line. There'll be quite a few stops until we get there."

The beach? Perfect.

And before I could even find a seat, the bus zoomed off.

Luckily, it wasn't packed, but because I was carrying a birdcage, I caught everyone's attention as I made my way down the aisle. I took a seat and told my bird, "You'll really like the beach," and since I hadn't been there all summer, I grinned.

"What kinda bird you got there?" the old man sitting across from me asked.

"It's a northern mockingbird," I answered.

"Kind of unusual for that kind of bird to be caged up, isn't it?"

"It only has one wing, so it can't fly, and it's in a cage to keep it safe."

"That's a shame. You plan on getting another bird to keep it company?"

I shrugged. "I dunno."

"Maybe a canary. I had a pretty little yellow one when I was a kid and loved to listen to it sing. Not sure if canaries and mockingbirds mix, but they're both songbirds, aren't they?"

"Yeah, they are," I replied, then stared at Hop, wondering when and if he'd ever sing.

As the bus rumbled down the street, I knew I should call my family and let them know I was safe, but I didn't have a cell phone yet because I'd been forbidden to have one until I turned twelve. It was after nine. By now, everyone would be worried, and them being worried wasn't cool. I needed to call—but who? If anyone was going to understand, it'd be G-Pop.

Before I asked a favor of the man who once had a canary, I studied him for a while. He seemed nice, like someone who probably wouldn't say no. "Sorry to bother you, mister, but do you have a phone I could use to call my grandpop? I just want to let him know I'm okay."

Suspicion filled his eyes.

"Please, mister," I begged. "Just one call."

Cautiously, he dug out his phone and handed it to me. "One call. That's all."

As a part of my emergency preparedness, I'd been forced to memorize certain phone numbers: Mom, Pops,

Nana, and G-Pop. I punched in his number. It only rang once before he picked up.

"G-Pop, it's me, Coop."

"Where—"

Before he could continue, I interrupted, "I'm okay. I just needed some time alone with Hop."

"They're worried," he said.

"I'm fine and I'll be home later. I have money too. You know, I am almost twelve. It's not like I'm a little kid."

The bus was coming to a stop, and the man who'd let me use his phone said, "My stop is coming up."

"Gotta go, G-Pop. I'll see you later. Don't worry." *Click.* "Thank you," I told the man as I handed him his phone.

"Everything alright?"

"Yes."

"By the way, where you headed?" he asked as he rose from his seat.

"Venice Beach," I replied.

He smiled. "Crowded there this time of year."

"Thanks again, mister, for letting me use your phone," I said as he headed to the exit door.

"Not a problem."

Two stops later, I stepped off the bus with my bird.

39

LIKE ALWAYS DURING the summer, the Venice Beach Boardwalk was crowded. There were jugglers and mimes, dogs on leashes dragging their owners along, and people who looked like tourists snapping pictures and selfies. Tattooed bodybuilders pumped iron while street performers who were half dancer and half acrobat worked hard to earn their dollars. Music blared. Above, squawking seabirds soared in the blue sky.

But soon Hop had my attention again. Was he as hungry as I was? Probably. I needed to get some berries, fruit, and water for him, and after that, a huge juicy burger and chili fries for me. Near the b-ball courts, I found everything I needed.

I was taking out the money to pay when the card the vet had given me fell on the ground. I picked it up, and this time, I read it. YOLANDA TOLIVER'S BIRD HAVEN, WILDLIFE REHABILITATOR, SANTA MONICA, CALIFORNIA. There was an address on Hightree Road, a phone number, and a picture of a woman with a bird perched on her shoulder. As I stuffed the card back into my pocket, racket from the courts caught my attention, and I headed over to check out some b-ball.

After putting water in the cage's container and scattering berries inside, I got busy with my burger and fries and watched the game.

They were shooting hoops, showing out, sweating under the summer sun. The game was lightning quick, and I knew that like all streetballers, they had their own set of rules. When one of them made a three-pointer, the audience, which now included me, cheered.

The crowd's buzz made me anxious to get back in the game, and I was picturing myself on the court when someone tapped me on the shoulder.

As soon as I turned around, a teenage girl got all up in my face to lecture me. "In case you didn't know, it's a crime to keep wild birds like mockingbirds as pets in cages. Birds need to fly. Plus, they deserve to be around other birds." Binoculars dangled from her neck.

For the second time today, I explained, "It's for his protection because he only has one wing and can't fly."

The fussy girl took a deep breath. "Sorry."

"Who are you supposed to be, anyway?" I asked. "The bird police?"

She plopped down beside me. "No, I'm a birder . . . some people call us bird watchers."

The binoculars, I realized, should have been my clue.

"I am too, well, sort of. We even made a bird sanctuary in my grandparents' backyard," I bragged.

She introduced herself. "My name's Jamie."

"I'm Coop."

"Which birder club do you belong to?" she asked.

Birder club? "None."

"Well, if you really like birds, and it seems like you do, you should join ours. It's called LAYB . . . Los Angeles Young Birders. We do a lot of fun things. If you're interested, all the info's online."

I smiled. "Thanks."

She stared at Hop. "Does your bird have a name?"

"Hop, his name is Hop."

"Really stinks that he has to be alone instead of with other birds."

"Yeah . . . it does."

We were still talking when a man heading toward us waved and called out, "Jamie!"

"That's my dad, I gotta go. Nice meeting you, Coop. Don't forget about Los Angeles Young Birders, LAYB. I'm the vice president."

"I won't," I promised.

As Jamie the birder strolled away alongside her dad and disappeared into the summertime crowd, I thought about two things: joining a birder club, which was cool, and Hop not being with other birds, which definitely wasn't.

I pulled the bird rehabilitator's card out of my pocket, looked at it again, and wondered where Hightree Road was and whether it was close enough to walk. Maybe I could at least go and see for myself. After all, it might be a really nice place. But what if it wasn't? No way was I leaving Hop in a dump with someone who was never going to care about him the way I did. What if she tried to force me and I had to make a second escape? I shook my head.

Cheers drew my attention back to the court. One of the players was showboating—beginning with a behind-the-back dribble, then a pump fake, followed by some change-of-pace dribbling, next a fast break, finishing with a reverse dunk. It reminded me of dancing, and I finally understood what Coach meant when he talked about the rhythm of basketball.

I don't know how long I stayed there watching, but I didn't leave till someone yelled, "Game over!"

40

AFTER WATCHING THE game, I picked up Hop's cage, made my way to the shore, and sat down in the warm sand. People strolled by, others waded in the water, and laughing kids splashed.

Seabirds were everywhere. Small ones hurried along, leaving paths of tiny footprints in the wet sand. Pelicans swooped and dived. Of course, noisy seagulls picked at the trash and seaweed. One even came right up to us and eyed Hop curiously. As if to say hello, Hop chirped and flapped his wing. The nosy seagull examined him for a while, then strutted off.

I was scanning the shoreline when I saw him, walking alone toward me—G-Pop.

"We're busted," I told Hop.

"How's my favorite grandson?" he asked as he sat down beside me.

As usual, I replied, "I'm your only grandson."

"And therefore, my favorite." And then, like always, we butted knuckles.

We both smiled, and then he made a call on his cell phone. "Found him . . . He's fine . . . No, I think we need to be alone for now. I'll see ya later."

"Who was that?" I asked.

"Your pops."

"How mad is he?"

G-Pop chuckled.

"How'd you find me, anyway?"

"The man who let you use the phone told me when I called his number back."

Rule number one when you're making a getaway, I thought, is never disclose your destination.

I shrugged and stared at my bird. "I wanted to keep him really bad."

He put his arm around my shoulder. "I know, Coop."

"But if I do, he'll mostly just be in a cage."

"That's true."

"And he won't be able to be with other birds."

"That's true too."

"And I really don't want to give him to that bird lady, but maybe if it's nice there, he'll have a better life. And maybe she'll even let me visit him sometimes."

He squeezed my shoulder. "Some decisions aren't easy, Coop . . . they just aren't. Sometimes this life business throws some curveballs. This has kind of been a summer of curveballs for you, hasn't it? So many unexpected things. The accident, the coma, a concussion, the broken arm, not being able to play b-ball, your bird almost dying . . ."

A summer of curveballs, that described it perfectly. "Yeah, it has been."

We stopped talking and sat there, watching the ocean. No matter what, G-Pop and I were always comfortable together.

After a while, G-Pop interrupted our quiet. "Always liked looking at the ocean, Coop, especially when it's kind of still and peaceful, the way it is now . . . has a way of making it seem like everything's gonna be alright."

"I wasn't running away," I explained again, then glanced at Hop. "I just wanted more time with him and some time to figure out what to do."

"And did you figure it out?"

I shrugged. "I dunno, maybe." I reached into my back

pocket, pulled out the bird lady's card, handed it to him, and asked, "How far away is it?"

G-Pop took out his phone and had the answer in seconds. "Not far . . . in Rustic Canyon."

"Can you take me there? I just want to see what it's like."

"Of course. But maybe we oughta call first, to let her know we're coming."

I agreed.

"And another thing, Coop."

"What?"

"You think Zandi should come along? She loves the little bird too."

I shrugged again.

"Is that a yes or a no?"

I stared at my bird. Zandi had known Hop for as long as I had, and except for one mistake, she'd taken good care of him. She'd even named him.

"It's a yes."

41

I was climbing into G-Pop's truck when he handed me the phone. "Call the lady with the aviary and see if it's okay for us to come by, Coop."

I punched in the number and a woman answered. "Yolanda Toliver's Bird Haven."

"Hi, Miz Toliver. The bird vet, Dr. Bloom, gave me your card—"

Before I could finish, she interrupted me. "You must be Coop. I've been expecting your call."

"We were wondering if we could come to see your . . . haven, in case I decide to let my bird live there."

"Can you get here before six?"

G-Pop gave a thumbs-up and said, "We have one stop to make before we head out your way. Give us an hour or so."

"See you soon. Bye, now."

Next, we called Nana to make sure Zandi would be ready.

While we drove, I started to think about what Pops calls repercussions. I figured after what I'd done, there'd definitely be some. "They're gonna ground me, huh?"

G-Pop chuckled. "Seems to me, with everything that's happened, you've already been grounded for most of the summer."

"For real, huh?"

I stared at Hop and thought of how this had been a summer of curveballs for him too. If he'd been born with two wings instead of one, he'd be soaring and exploring like the others he'd shared the nest with, and probably singing too. Instead, here he was, only chirping now and then, all alone in his cage. Suddenly, that side of the coin where I somehow got to keep my bird disappeared, and the only side left was the one where I did what was best for Hop. I really wanted him to be happy, and right then I decided that if this Bird Haven was a nice place and I could visit him sometimes, I'd let him stay there.

G-Pop must have read my mind. "Hard even thinking about giving up something you care about, isn't it?"

I nodded, and a few minutes of sad silence followed.

But after being quiet for a while, I told him about the birder girl, Jamie, and the club she belonged to, Los Angeles Young Birders.

"That something that interests you?"

"Yeah, it is."

42

ZANDI AND NANA were waiting outside when we pulled up to the curb. Nana smiled at me, but Zandi looked upset.

She slid into the truck beside me, stared at Hop, and said, "Hey, Hop." Then she turned to me. "You're giving him away to some person I never heard of without even telling me? He's not just your bird, Coop. He's mine too. Plus, you got to spend time alone with him today and I didn't. It's not fair!"

I offered my best defense—"It's probably what's best for Hop"—but it wasn't good enough, and she kept on.

"Says who? You? You're not the only one who loves Hop! I love him too!"

That Zandi loved Hop was true, and I started to feel bad that she didn't get to spend the day with him like I had. And right then I realized that I, Coop Garnette, had only been thinking about myself. I really meant it when I told her, "Sorry, Zandi."

Her reply was a teary-eyed stare.

Seconds later, G-Pop pressed his foot on the gas, and we were off.

It was a tree-lined street. "This is it," G-Pop said as we pulled up in front of a house with lots of windows.

The four of us walked up to the front door, which opened before we could even ring the bell. "Hi, I'm Yolanda, or, as some people call me around here, the Bird Lady." She zeroed in on me and grinned. "You must be Coop."

"Yes," I replied, and introduced her to G-Pop, Nana, and Zandi. Then I held up the cage for her to see. "And this is Hop."

"Hello, Hop," the Bird Lady said, and welcomed us inside. "Follow me."

We trailed her through the house and into the back-yard. Our bird sanctuary was nothing compared to this. This yard, which had a huge pond, was amazing.

"Isn't that Rustic Canyon Park back there?" Nana asked.

"Yes, it is. It's the reason we bought this house. Even though the birds aren't exactly free, we wanted them to have the feeling that they were."

G-Pop grinned. "Kind of like a five-star hotel for birds."

"We do our best. Let me show you the aviaries."

There were three, she explained, each housing compatible birds. "The last thing we want is for any bird to harm another. Most are only temporary guests, and once they're ready or healed, they'll be released into the wild. But others, for various reasons, will live here permanently."

"Like Hop, maybe?" I asked.

"Yes."

Birds in the aviaries were singing, chattering, chirping, sounding like they were happy.

Zandi, who'd been quiet, finally spoke up. "It's really pretty here, but I have a question. Are there any other mockingbirds?"

"As a matter of fact, there's an older female with a broken wing that's healing. She'll be here for a while until it gets better. And I have a few other birds who, like Hop, only have one wing, mostly from injuries or being attacked by predators."

I took a deep breath. Everything about this place seemed better than Hop being caged up at G-Pop and Nana's. "Could we come to visit him sometimes?"

"As you can imagine, the haven keeps me pretty busy. Once a week works for me. As long as you call first." She paused. "So you've decided?"

I looked at Zandi and asked her, "What do you think?"

After she nodded, I took another deep breath and said, "Okay."

The Bird Lady commended me and Zandi for taking such good care of him. "Hop is one lucky bird," she said. "Most who are like him don't survive. You two did a good thing."

It felt good when the Bird Lady said that and Zandi smiled at me. One look into her eyes told me that we were friends again.

Then it was time to let Hop go.

As soon as I reached inside the cage, he hopped into my hand. I petted him, and then Zandi held him, and then it was my turn again.

"You're gonna be happy here. And we won't forget

about you, and I promise we'll come back to see you . . . I promise." Hop chirped and flapped his wing.

By now, Zandi was crying.

"I'll take very good care of him," the Bird Lady said as she opened the aviary door.

As I handed Hop to her, I whispered, "See ya next week, little dude."

43

Mom and Pops were standing in the open doorway, look-ing very displeased, when G-Pop dropped me off at home.

"I'm sorry," I told my parents.

"Coop, look at me!" Pops commanded. "Do . . . not . . . ever . . . do . . . anything . . . like . . . that . . . again!" he said sternly.

"I won't . . . I said sorry and I really am. But I just gave away my bird. You could at least take pity on me."

That seemed to calm him down, and when we stepped inside, I detected some sympathy in their eyes. Pops gently touched my shoulder.

Mom offered me a hug and afterward had tears in her eyes. "This has been some kind of summer," she told me.

Pops chimed in, "First the accident and now this little stunt."

Little stunt? "I just needed time to think. Can I go to my room now?"

They glanced at each other and said, "Yes."

"Is the bird place where you left him nice?" Mom asked.

"Yeah, real nice. He'll be safe there," I replied. Still carrying the birdcage, I headed to my cave and plopped onto my bed.

I was already missing Hop. Leaving him there was the right thing to do, wasn't it? But—it sure wasn't easy. Right then, I wanted to go back and get him, but I'd made my decision and there was no changing it now.

I thought about my birth mother and wondered if that was why she'd left me at the hospital that day. Maybe it wasn't because she didn't love me. Maybe it was because she did.

44

Two days later, I trudged up the stairs to G-Pop's. Even though Hop was gone, there was work to be done in the sanctuary, and I'd been summoned.

As soon as I walked in, I zeroed in on Hop's empty cage.

G-Pop, of course, noticed. "I've sure been missing that bird. Never realized how much joy our little houseguest had brought into our lives."

He was right. Nana was busy in the kitchen and Zandi was on the balcony, looking out over the backyard. But something was missing, and that something was Hop.

When Zandi came inside, our sad eyes met.

G-Pop filled in the silence. "So, last time I checked, the sanctuary had your names on it, and the other birds out there still deserve your attention, don't they?"

We both replied yes.

"The hummingbird feeders are almost out of nectar, the bird feeders need seed, and the birdbath could use a scrubbing and fresh water." He glanced at the wall clock, grabbed his clubs, and headed to the door. "I'm late for my golf game," he said. "You two have fun."

Fun? Fun was the last thing on my mind, and from the look on Zandi's face, it was the last thing on hers too.

Silently, we refilled the hummingbird feeder that hung from the balcony, and in no time two hummingbirds were hovering.

Then we grabbed supplies and headed outside to our sanctuary. Birds were here and there, chirping to one another, and when Nana began playing her cello up on the balcony, music was everywhere.

Zandi and I had just put fresh water in the birdbath when she said, "Remember the first time Hop got in the water and he was flapping his wing?"

I'd never forget. "Yeah, he was so happy."

My mind flooded with so many memories—watching

the eggs hatch one by one, the day we discovered that he only had one wing, the way we'd rescued and fed him, trying to teach him to sing.

When a bird landed in the birdbath, she said, "It's really pretty, huh? Wonder what kind it is?"

"Dunno." I'd never seen one like that, I thought, or had I? Until those mockingbirds had built their nest in G-Pop's tree, I really hadn't paid much attention to birds. But after taking care of Hop, I knew I'd never ignore them again, and I suddenly remembered Jamie, the birder girl at Venice Beach.

"I almost forgot to tell you. I met this girl at the beach who belongs to a birder club for kids. It's called Los Angeles Young Birders, LAYB, and she said they do some fun stuff and she wants me to join."

"Are you going to?"

"I think so. You should too. It sounds interesting."

Zandi shrugged, but her eyes were kind of warming up.

I gazed into the tree. "You think some birds will build another nest?"

"Maybe. Especially now that we made the sanctuary." Then her voice turned serious. "Just remember one thing, Coop."

"What?"

"Don't ever go climbing up there again, because next time, you might not be so lucky."

I glanced at my scarred arm and knew she was right. I'd learned my lesson. "I won't," I promised.

She got a serious look and stared straight into my eyes. "I know you wish you hadn't fallen and gotten hurt, and so do I. The best thing that happened is you're okay, but the best thing we did was saving Hop."

I knew what Zandi meant. Saving a bird with just one wing probably seemed like a small thing or a waste of time to most people, but to us, it wasn't a small thing or a waste of time. Like G-Pop said, love is never a waste of time.

45

As PROMISED, WE had made our weekly visits to the Bird Haven, and each time, Hop seemed happy to see us. Almost a month had passed, and visiting day had come again. We rang the buzzer at the side entrance, and when the Bird Lady opened the side gate, she had a bigger smile than usual. "I have some very good news for you," she told us.

"What?" I asked.

"Number one, that older female mockingbird has taken a special liking to Hop, and even after so much human contact, he seems to have taken a liking to her." She kept talking as we trailed behind her. "And number two, Hop is singing."

It was what I'd been waiting for. I sprinted toward the aviary, and Zandi was right behind me.

"Coop and Zandi!" G-Pop called out. "Slow down! Be careful!"

I peered into the aviary. Where was he?

"Can we go inside?" I asked Yolanda when she and G-Pop caught up.

Carefully, she opened the door and let Zandi and me in. "He's found a favorite hangout right around here." She found him in no time. "And there he is."

I knelt down so he could see me, and as soon as I said, "Hey, little dude," he hopped toward me.

"He still remembers me!" I exclaimed. Week after week, I'd been amazed that he hadn't forgotten me and hoped he never would.

"Mockingbirds have very good memories," the Bird Lady reminded me.

In no time, he'd hopped into my cupped hands.

Gently, I handed him to Zandi. "Hey, Hop," she told him.

And that was when he did it. He flapped his wing and tweeted a birdsong, some of the prettiest music I'd ever heard. "Wow! He's a really good singer, isn't he?"

Everyone agreed.

Before we left, I told the Bird Lady, "Thank you. This is way better than him being in a cage. He seems really happy here."

"Thank *you*, Coop," Yolanda replied. "Giving up something we love because we know it's the best thing to do takes courage."

On the drive home, I thought a lot about what Yolanda had said. And I asked myself, *How much courage had it taken for my birth mother to bring me to the hospital that day?*

46

Months Later

MY SUMMER OF curveballs was over. Coop Garnette and his one-winged mockingbird had both survived.

School had started, and Zandi and I were about to take our third bird-watching trip with the Los Angeles Young Birders. We'd also continued our visits to see Hop, who was growing and always impressed us with new songs. "You might never fly," I told him, "but you sure can sing."

After everything that had gone wrong, some things had definitely gone right. Hop was happy and in a safe place, and I was back on the court with the Meteors. Week after week my b-ball skills were improving, but sadly, my confidence wasn't.

Game night had finally arrived. I glanced over at

Mom, Pops, G-Pop, and Nana, the Garnettes, sitting side by side in the bleachers. They rarely missed one of my games.

Because it was the first game of the season, it kind of surprised me when Coach let me play. Was I about to embarrass myself and my team? My right wrist still hurt sometimes. Maybe I'd try shooting left-handed, the way Pops and I had been practicing.

I was near the top of the key, just outside the three-point line, when Mason passed me the ball. "You got this, Coop," he said. "Take the shot!"

I dribbled and thought, *I hope he's right.* "This one's for you, Hop," I said as I focused on the net and, with my left hand, shot the ball. When it hit the backboard, I cringed. What was I thinking, trying to show out? The ball circled the rim. "Please go in. Please," I whispered.

The ball must have heard me, because that's exactly what it did. My second three-pointer ever.

The Garnettes were on their feet, and my team was cheering.

Coop Garnette was back in the game!

Author's Note

BECAUSE OF THE circumstances and timing of my birth, my mother did not feel she was capable of caring for me. Shortly after I was born, I was offered to a couple for adoption. The reasons why my mother later decided against the adoption are unclear and not something she ever chose to disclose. She is now deceased, and I will never know.

I was an adult when I learned this part of my life story. She did tell me that the couple were unable to have biological children, that the woman was a teacher, that they were financially secure, and that they and the woman's parents wanted me desperately.

My childhood with my mother was complicated, and I spent time in foster care. Often, throughout my life, I have found myself wondering how different it might have been had my mother gone through with the adoption. Would my childhood have been better or worse? I will never know.

With Just One Wing grew from this life event, and as I wrote, I consciously gave Coop the parents and grandparents I would have chosen for myself.

Adoption, like life, will certainly have its ups and downs, and adopting a child comes with a unique set of challenges; it should never be entered into lightly. There are questions that may or may not have answers. Adoptees, like all children, deserve love. Love—that amazing, transformative emotion.

Coop's story is the story of one young adoptee with a lot of questions, some of which are answered by his love for a little bird with just one wing. It is just one story, one story out of millions, one story about redemption and belonging and love.

Acknowledgments

EVERY BOOK IS a collaborative effort. There are many people who made *With Just One Wing* possible, and I thank them all. I am especially grateful to:

Nancy Paulsen for sharing my vision and for her finely tuned guidance and skillful editing. Additional thanks go to Sara LaFleur and everyone behind the scenes at Nancy Paulsen Books.

Nadia Fisher for her amazing art for the jacket. It is beyond my expectations. Thank you, Nadia.

Cindy Howle for her careful, thoughtful, and meticulous copyediting.

Clinical psychologist Rochelle Bastien, PhD, for her

insights about adoption. I have known this gifted woman since we were in the third grade. Thank you, Rochelle.

The National Wildlife Federation and the U.S. Fish and Wildlife Service for everything they do to protect at-risk wildlife. Thank you.

Everyone at Penguin Random House who worked to make sure *With Just One Wing* made it from that quiet space in my mind into the hands of readers. Thank you.

As always, I thank the Spirit for its gentle guidance.